A Ghost of a Clue

by

Debra Doggett

Lobster Cove Series

A Ghost of a Clue

Cover Art by *Tina Lynn Stout*

The Wild Rose Press, Inc.
PO Box 708
Adams Basin, NY 14410-0708
Visit us at www.thewildrosepress.com

Publishing History
First Faery Rose Edition, 2014
Digital ISBN 978-1-62830-684-2
Print ISBN 978-1-62830-860-0

Lobster Cove Series
Published in the United States of America

Rory blew out a breath.

"If I tell you yes, I'm messing with you when I say there were ghosts here tonight then you're okay with that. You're comfortable with it. If I tell you no, that there really was a ghost, two in fact, here tonight, then the train derails and you run for the hills."

He stared at her for a moment with a thoughtful look on his face. "Tell me what you believe you saw."

"The truth?"

Travis nodded. "The truth of what you believe you saw."

"That's a very guarded way of putting it."

"No. It's a very scientific way of putting it. I can't know what to think if I don't have all the evidence."

"Fair enough. I saw two ghosts."

"Whole images?"

"One fairly solid, a little boy and one kind of wavering, an older woman."

He watched her face as she said it, and Rory held her breath, waiting for the sneer that had always accompanied any talk of her gift in the past. She would be sorry to see him walk away. Even though it had only been a few weeks, she realized she'd come to enjoy his company. Part of her knew she'd been hoping for something more, no matter how much she told herself she wasn't going to do another relationship. Still, it would hurt, and she steeled herself for the good-bye. At last he nodded.

"Okay, you saw two ghosts."

"You're not headed for the door."

"The kids aren't packed up yet." He grinned. "And the train is still on the tracks, Ms. DuMont. Nothing's derailed yet."

Dedication

To those who walk outside the box.
May your journeys be exciting.

Chapter One

"Aurora DuMont?"

"Yes." Rory smiled at the older woman as she wondered for the third time why in the world she had agreed to come tonight. She was so not a people person. The idea that this many folks would willingly gather together once a month to talk to each other about anything was beyond her ability to understand. Yet here she stood, still trying to decipher how her fast talking neighbor had gotten her to agree to this.

KS Bennson was a crotchety old man who had clearly spent too much time in his own lighthouse. He had a need to talk like most people needed to eat. Cornered as she was taking a walk along the coastline, Rory had listened politely as KS gushed with excitement over the Lobster Cove Ghost Hunters Society. In the first fifteen minutes, she'd learned about all the ghost sightings in Lobster Cove for the last fifty years. She still couldn't figure out how, but by the end of the conversation, she'd agreed to come and talk to the society about her own experiences with the paranormal, a detail of her life she had determined to keep quiet about while she was in Lobster Cove. The old man was sneaky, she'd give him that.

"It is so nice to meet you." The woman she suspected was Jane Harvitz, president of the society, beamed at her. KS's description had been rather detailed. Rory suspected her neighbor had a slight crush on Jane.

"Thank you, Ms. Harvitz. I appreciate the chance to get to know some folks in Lobster Cove."

"Please call me Jane. Lorena was a wonderful woman, very spirited and outspoken. You take after her a bit around the face."

Rory thought back to her father's description of her great-aunt Lorena DuMont. It had been much less flattering and far more blunt. According to him, Rory not only took after Aunt Lorena in looks, but in personality as well. Outspoken was not high on her father's list of acceptable attributes for women, and Aunt Lorena was not high on his list of family favorites. If her letters were any indication, the feeling was mutual. Had her father known about the part of Rory's heritage that Aunt Lorena had taught her to use, there would have been open war between the two of them.

"Thank you." Rory smiled at her. "She was very kind to me. I miss her so much. It's been a bit of a transition moving clear across the country."

"That cottage was her passion. From the day she moved in, she made it one of the most beautiful spots in town. We all feared it would be left to rot after she passed, what with her having no husband or children of her own. Now it will be lived in and loved by you."

The old cottage had been a fixture in Lobster Cove since the 1920s, when it was built by the captain of a whaler who had decided he'd had enough of living on the sea. He'd been an old man by then and never had a family so the cottage was small but cozy. The story went that he'd built the place by the shore because he couldn't sleep without the sound of the waves crashing. In spite of its location, the story also alleged he never walked the shore, preferring instead to sit in front of the cottage and watch the people of the town. The old man was tougher than even he'd thought for he lived in the tiny cottage for nearly twenty years. After his death it had stood empty for almost a decade before her aunt had purchased it, renovating it in a style that likely had the old captain spinning in his grave.

"I have to admit I was surprised she passed *Maison de la Mer* to me." Rory laughed. "With such a fancy name, I don't know if I can live up to it."

"Ah, Lorena believed everything should have a name. Or a title, as she called it. And that's what the place was to her, her Home by the Sea. Leave it to her to fancy it up a bit, just like she did with that old place. We're all excited to get you settled in and a part of Lobster Cove."

Rory didn't want to disappoint her hostess with the news that her stay in Lobster Cove was meant to be temporary, so she just smiled. The cottage had been a godsend. Right before the letter came from Aunt Lorena's attorney; her whole life seemed to have taken a tumble. Her job at the Colorado Historical Society fell victim to budget cuts, and her relationship with Jerrod fell victim to a scheming ex-girlfriend. She'd needed a place to recoup, and spending a few months in Lobster Cove sounded like just the thing to get her life back on track.

"We're also so glad you're here tonight to defend the truth for us."

"Defend the truth?" Warning bells went off in Rory's head. "I'm afraid—"

"We're all so pleased to have someone articulate and knowledgeable on our side of this debate. Richard and I worried over how we were going to approach this ever since the whole business came up at the last city council meeting."

"Debate?"

"Not that Mr. Reed is a horrible person or anything. He certainly isn't. I mean, he's not going to insult you or be rude. It's just that he's such a skeptic when it comes to the supernatural. And after the last little incident, he just doesn't want to let it go. I understand it's his job, but he could be a bit more open-minded about things. Who knew scientists were so hard-headed?"

"Mr. Reed?"

Rory was beginning to feel a bit like a parrot. Or a lamb being led to the slaughter. She would've backed up to the door but the woman had her arm in an iron grip and was already moving her toward the living room. What in the world had polite conversation gotten her into now, she wondered. Before she could spy out another exit, her gaze landed on the room full of people, all of them looking at her with what could only be described as expectation. Of what she wasn't certain but her intuition was already shouting that she wouldn't like it.

Jane maneuvered her to the podium set up in front of the fireplace, never taking her firm grip off Rory's arm. She had caught her prey, and she wasn't letting go, Rory thought with a sense of resignation. Maybe the snacks would be worth it. As they neared the man standing by the podium, Rory felt a ray of hope that maybe something beyond the snacks would be worth her visit tonight. Her inner voice reminded her she had sworn off relationships, but she told it to shut up. Besides, she reassured it, casual sex didn't involve a relationship. So long as she kept things casual, she would be safe, and she would have fun. Fun and relaxation were what she had come to Lobster Cove for after all. And the man standing in front of her looked like loads of fun. Before her vivid imagination could elaborate any more on her fantasy, her hostess introduced her.

"Aurora DuMont, this is Travis Reed."

A bit disappointed at having her fantasy exploded so soon, Rory found herself tilting her head. It was rare for her to find someone tall enough to make her do that. So this was the man who wasn't going to insult her, Rory thought, as she took in her unexpected adversary. Travis Reed wasn't only tall, he looked Viking big. If his red hair had been longer and his clothing a bit more barbaric, he could pass as a Norseman. Still the broad shoulders underneath the dark suit impressed the hell out of her, and the way the suit fit him looked yummy. As a matter of fact, all of him looked yummy especially the wild blue eyes that stared at her with a bit of amusement in them. Rory wanted to sigh as her inner voice screeched out a warning. She had come here to find some balance, not to sign up for yet another inappropriate relationship. And a hardheaded scientist sounded like a tough sell for a woman who saw ghosts. Still, he had a killer smile that lit up more than the room as he reached out a hand to her.

"Hello, Ms. DuMont. Nice to finally meet the talk of the town."

His voice rumbled out of the suit in a friendly

baritone. Rory frowned, but she didn't hear any insult behind the casual words. Lobster Cove seemed quaint and cozy, but all small towns came with gossip. That much she knew from experience. Gossip wasn't on her agenda, especially when it concerned her. She froze her most polite smile on her face and decided to forego her lustful fantasies and nip the conversation in the bud.

"I'm sorry, Mr. Reed, but you have me at a loss. You seem to know quite a bit about me, but other than your name, I know nothing of you. And I only learned your name a few minutes before I found out we were having this little debate tonight, which I'm a bit confused about."

"Feeling like a Christian being thrown to the lions, huh?" He ignored her snarky tone and grinned at her with unrepentant glee. From the look on his face, he was having the time of his life. That made it hard to keep the smile from her own face.

"Except I guess you'd be the one they burn at the stake instead." He looked her up and down, and Rory found she was glad she'd dressed up tonight. "Though I must say you don't live up to the image of the stereotypical witch."

"Excuse me?" Her self-confidence backpedaling, Rory frowned up at him.

"You know, all the pictures. Long riotous red curls, wild, sexy clothes, all that."

Rory couldn't believe she had left home tonight for this. KS was going to have some explaining to do the next time they talked. Instead of sharing a few stories, she'd been set-up to debate someone who looked like her fantasy dream date, and now, said fantasy was insulting her before they'd exchanged more than a few words. She smoothed a hand down her straight brown locks, remembering how pleased she'd been with the short do knowing it would be so much easier to fix. And her conservative blue dress had been a concession to her assumption about the age of the group members. So much for trying to blend in.

"Um, I mean, not that you don't look lovely."

Travis Reed must have noticed the look on her face and realized the impact of his words. The glee disappeared from his face, and now he looked like a man who'd swallowed his tongue. Rory stifled a laugh.

"I mean, your dress is really pretty, you look great, just not…"

"Sexy?"

"Uh…I don't know that I'd go that far."

"You've already gone pretty far, Mr. Reed, so why stop now? You know though—" Rory tapped a finger on her chin "—if we're going for stereotypes, I'm thinking you should be the witch instead of me."

"What?"

The confusion on his face was laughable. If not compliments, Rory thought, I'll settle for a bit of fun. It wasn't casual sex but it was better than nothing.

"Well, you fit the stereotype and you're right, I don't."

"I…what…?"

Rory found herself wishing she'd renewed her first aid card. He looked like he was going to choke on that tongue he'd swallowed. But she couldn't resist twisting the knife a bit more.

"I'm betting there would be some riotous curls if you let that red hair of yours grow out."

"Which is exactly why I never will," he mumbled.

Then his face brightened. "Hey, wait a minute, does that mean you think I'm sexy, too?"

Rory stifled a groan. Of course he'd catch on to that. She should've been more cautious. It had been too long since she'd bantered with a man who had a brain in his head. Time to move on, she thought.

"I think we should save the sparring for the debate. Shame about the hair, though. Now maybe we should call it a draw and go find the snack table and take some time to regroup. Both of us need to be prepared since I believe we're the entertainment for tonight. I can work on my image, and you can untangle your tongue. Then we can have a go at each other again, Mr. Reed."

"Let me apologize first. And call me Travis, please. I'm not in class."

She gave him a quizzical look. "In class? Are you a student?"

"Nope." He grinned. "I'm the teacher. A science teacher to be exact. I teach biology, botany, and general science at Lobster Cove Middle School."

"Middle school? And you talk about me going into the lion's den?"

Travis laughed. "At least you would be the captive victim. It shows you're the smarter one. I walked in willingly. Some days I even walk back out in one piece."

"But not of sound mind?"

"Not at all. Perfect evidence of that is the fact that I walk back in there the next day."

"Sad to see a good mind go to waste."

"So you think I have a good mind to start with? And will that hold true after I debunk your ghost hunting?'

"You so sure you can do that?"

"I'm a middle school science teacher. I'm used to arguing with emotion."

"Oh, so my argument will be all emotion, and yours will be all logic and reason, huh?"

"Uh, I think I'd like to go back to flirting with you and, like you said, save the arguing for the debate."

"That was your idea of flirting?"

"I spend eight hours a day with preteens, so yeah that was my juvenile attempt at flirting with you."

"I'm feeling better about the debate then. Your communication skills pretty much suck."

"Glad I could help give you a sense of overconfidence. That was my strategy all along."

"Uh-huh."

He offered her his arm. "Why don't we check out those snacks like you said? Jane's spread is the finest kind, so maybe I can help you fill your plate and thereby send you into a food coma. I like to take every tactic I can to ensure my success."

Rory laid her hand on his sleeve and tried to ignore the tingle of energy that touching him gave her. No entanglements, she sternly reminded herself. "Is there wine at the table?"

"Nope. I already checked, right after Jane told me about the debate."

"So you didn't know about it till you got here either?"

"No. I figured I was invited so they could spend the meeting roasting me at the stake for getting the city council to calm down over the ghost sightings in the old city hall. It took a full half hour speech to convince them they didn't need to use city funds to cordon off the county clerk's office until they could get the whole area ritually cleansed with some special ceremony. That's why I was glad to hear of your, um, beliefs. I figured they might roast you first, and I could run away while they were distracted."

"There are ghosts in city hall?" She almost laughed at the look of frustration that came over his face.

"No. That was my point."

"And that's what we're going to debate?"

"God, I hope not. I'm kind of tired of talking about it. I think we're going to be more general."

"More general?"

"You know, do ghosts exist? That kind of stuff."

"Piece of cake."

"You think so, huh? Well, I have to warn you I come prepared."

"So much the better. Though I have to confess I am surprised you came at all with an attitude like yours. I would think at a meeting of a ghost-hunting society you'd be sort of outnumbered. You never know. This might be a tougher crowd than your classroom."

"Actually, being here is probably easier than my classroom. They're a whole lot nicer to me."

"Really?"

"Maybe I should say they're more polite and better at hiding what they think. At least they listen to me. They aren't trying to text on their phones while I'm talking."

"Kids actually use their phones during your class?"

"I have a few who can hardly put the damn things down without having them surgically removed. And, a few who think they invented smooth moves never before known to man so they can fool a poor dumb teacher."

"Smooth moves?"

"They harbor the crazy belief that a teacher can't tell that a kid who's spent the last ten minutes looking at his crotch and smiling is texting."

"Sounds like you're used to staying on your toes. I don't know though." Rory glanced around the room as she filled one of the small plates with fruit. "I'm betting you won't be competing with cell phones here. And you can't yell at them if you are. No grades to threaten them with either. You have to be polite and hide what you're thinking, too. This might be tougher than you're prepared for. You'll have to keep it interesting or you'll lose them."

"Always. I do interesting very well."

I'll bet you do, thought Rory before reminding herself that she wasn't into interesting anymore. She'd come to Lobster Cove for balance and harmony and that's what she was sticking with, no matter what her hormones screamed for.

"You two look awfully chummy for debate opponents. Are you working up what line of bunk to tell these fools?"

Rory didn't recognize the slightly inebriated woman weaving her way toward them, but Travis must have from the groan he managed to smother. It looked like someone had found the wine. Or, maybe drank it all before others could get to it. She looked to be in her late fifties, maybe early sixties. It was hard to tell for the years hadn't been kind. Rumpled clothing hung on the woman's thin frame, and her lean face wore what looked to be a perpetual frown.

"Hi, Margaret." Travis looked like he'd stolen her

fake smile. "Did you come to cheer me on?"

The woman gave an inelegant snort. "Not hardly. I always come to these things. Somebody's got to keep tabs on the crazies from both sides."

"From both sides?" Rory reached out a hand to steady the woman before she fell into the table. A tingle of energy of a much less pleasant kind hit her as soon as they touched. Rory withdrew her hand.

"Margaret believes in ghosts. She just doesn't believe in ghost hunters. Margaret Vincent, this is Aurora DuMont. She's Lorena's niece, and she's living in the cottage now."

The woman gave Travis a withering glance. "I keep up with the gossip, too." She turned an even more withering stare on Rory. "I know all about the witch who's moved into town."

Rory struggled to roll out her polite manners. "Wow, and I was afraid I'd have to spend weeks getting to know everyone. Guess I'll have to get used to how word gets around in a small town. And it's Rory. Aurora sounds a bit too celestial."

She extended her hand to Margaret, who ignored both it and her comments. Though she'd promised to keep her intuition in check tonight, Rory couldn't help taking a glimpse at the woman's aura. Something about her gave off some really strange vibes. That kind of hostility from someone she had just met usually came with issues on their side. After only a few seconds, she shut her third eye down. Drunk or not, this Margaret had some serious disturbance going on under the surface, and it didn't all come from alcohol. The dirty mustard-colored shadow around her radiated pain in pulsing waves.

Rory worried for a minute that she was losing her touch when it came to surreptitious snooping. Margaret glared at her as if she knew what Rory had done, and she wasn't happy about it. Then the look was gone. What replaced it wasn't any friendlier, but at least her expression didn't have the outright venom it had before.

"I don't believe, I know for a fact." Margaret peered at her through bloodshot eyes, and Rory felt a shiver run along her spine. "I've seen ghosts, seen them up close and personal."

For a moment Rory thought Margaret had seen inside her as well. Something in the disdain on her face gave more meaning to her words than the surface would indicate. But then her expression twisted back into a sneer.

"And a bunch of idiots running around with cameras and weird-ass doodads aren't ever going to see them. Ghosts would laugh in their faces." With that pronouncement she stumbled off, leaving Rory curious and a bit relieved.

"Well, that was fun."

"Yeah." Travis nodded. "Margaret's always a great addition to any gathering. You can think of it as a warm-up for the rest of tonight's entertainment."

"I'm hoping the rest of our audience is a bit more congenial."

"You hang on to that hope." Travis held out his arm to her. "I see Jane's waving everyone to their seats. Looks like we're up."

Not sure that she wanted to touch anyone again, Rory laid a careful arm on his and really hoped she was up for this.

Chapter Two

I've got to get used to the sea spray, at least while I'm here, Rory thought as the mist pelted her. Running along the coast was becoming her morning routine. It gave her the chance to see the rolling waves and connect with the creatures that played there. When she first arrived in the small town, she'd followed her long habit of introducing herself to the native spirits of the land and water. Lobster Cove's elemental community was a playful one.

Sitting for morning meditations, however, was a habit Rory had never been able to develop, in spite of all Aunt Lorena's efforts. Moving stimulated her senses far better, and she'd discovered in the few weeks she'd been here that the pounding waves were wonderful background noise for opening her chakras. She wondered if she would be able to keep running once the sea mist mingled with the winter chill. It was the first week in October, and already she noticed the change. Fall colors enchanted her senses, but she'd lived in Denver for enough years to know how fast they could change to winter white. Once winter really hit, she'd probably wimp out on her runs and turn into a couch potato for the duration. Hibernating indoors with a stack of old movies and an endless supply of junk food might not be a good moving meditation technique, but it was a great way to hole up and heal. She'd come here to relax, after all. It would give her the quiet and the isolation she'd told herself she'd find in the little Maine town.

Thinking about potential relationships had her mind wandering back to last night. She smiled as she thought back to the surprise debate. In her own humble opinion, she'd run circles around Travis Reed's logical and unemotional arguments against the possibility of the existence of ghosts. Of course, she'd been playing to a more sympathetic audience. Still, her personal touch had them eating out of her hand. It was the first interaction of any depth she'd had with the locals, and she thought it went stunningly well. She'd told a few stories they enjoyed, and nothing went beyond the surface of common ghost-hunter lore. Now if she could manage to stay away from any more conversations with her enthusiastic neighbor, she might never have to do it again.

Rory headed down the path that led to the center of town. She'd never dared run along the highway back in Denver but the streets in Lobster Cove felt much safer. Maybe it was the fact that there were about a million less cars on them. It had been a long time since she'd been out of the big city. Rory had to admit it was a nice feeling.

The long stretch of highway melted into the pretty town square where the fall colors were even more beautiful. She slowed to a walk to cool down as she passed the yard of a plantation-style house that had to be one of the older structures in Lobster Cove. Birch trees with shimmering red-gold leaves dotted the lawn, creating the perfect scene of fall color. Her artist's eye honed in on it and filed it away for a later visit when she had her camera with her. Years of working as a graphic artist for museum exhibits and displays were her ace in the hole for self-employment. At least that was what she'd been telling herself since she'd arrived here. The beauty of the Maine coast and of Lobster Cove itself would work nicely on postcards and prints, things she could design with her now unemployed time.

As she rounded the front of the building, she noticed the name on the heavy front door. The Shucker's Booktique. Clever, she thought. A glance through the window told her it was a place that needed a longer look. From what she saw, it held the potential to be a boon for the business she had in mind. She glanced down at her ratty running attire and decided an introduction to the owner should wait until she was more impressively dressed. Just because she was unemployed didn't mean she needed to look like it.

Her stroll took her down the sidewalk opposite the Booktique as she perused the other assorted businesses lining the town square. There were some interesting places, and she mentally planned a shopping day as she walked along. It couldn't hurt to get to know some more folks in town, especially if she wanted to make some business contacts.

One window caught her eye and her appetite. Poorly dressed or not, Rory told herself she'd earned one of the mouthwatering little pastries filling the case in the window. Surely she'd run long enough to indulge in just one. That was her story and she was sticking to it, she told herself as she walked past the window and through the door of Sweet Bea's.

It was like walking into everyone's fantasy idea of their grandmother's kitchen, all warm and homey. Even the air smelled sweet, although with the aroma from the collection of goodies sitting there, waiting to be devoured, Rory didn't see how it could smell like anything else.

The place was busy, with all three tables occupied along with two of the five stools at the counter. The tiny bell on the door kept up a steady ringing. A red-haired beauty behind the counter was busy flirting with an attractive guy in a park ranger uniform. Rory took advantage of her distraction to browse the cases. There in lie every kind of decadent pastry her imagination could have imagined, from giant iced cookies to elegantly frosted cupcakes and a hefty slice of what was labeled vanilla cake with raspberry filling. With a reluctant sigh, she let her gaze wander past the vanilla cake with the promise of a longer run and a slice of it later. She compromised on a cinnamon scone, telling herself it was at least reasonably healthy.

"Come on, you're not really going to settle for something without frosting, are you? After last night I'd have thought you were braver than that."

Rory turned like a kid caught with her hand in the cookie jar. She raised a brow at Travis, who stood grinning at her. The suit was gone, replaced by worn jeans and a black T-shirt that said "Maine Attraction" in big bold letters. Underneath the words was a grinning lobster wearing sunglasses. He still looked yummy.

"I don't like to think of it as settling. I like to think of it as a responsible, logical choice in the pursuit of good nutrition."

He shook his head. "Nothing in Bea's cases fits that description. If you're looking for food that follows the arbitrary rules of nutrition, you need to come to the school cafeteria. They are firm believers in no frosting there."

"Dispassionate, logical and unemotional believers?"

"Yes, ma'am. They don't even have a passion for cooking. It's just part of the job for them. Now Bea on the other hand—" he waved a hand at the redhead behind the counter "—has got cooking down to an art."

"So I should choose carefully, is that what you're telling me?"

"If it were me I'd choose one of each. I've found that usually works out best."

"Ah, but you have a classroom full of preteens to help you work it off. I, on the other hand, have to run an extra mile for every tablespoon of frosting."

"Are you trying to argue my customer out of her purchase, Travis?"

The redhead smiled up at him as she walked over.

"Not at all, Bea. I'm trying to argue her into buying the whole damn case."

"And sharing a goodly portion with you, is that your plan?" She leaned over the counter and stuck a hand out to Rory. "I'm Bea, Beatrice O'Brien. Welcome to Sweet Bea's."

"Rory. Rory DuMont."

"Ah, Lorena's niece. Welcome to Lobster Cove."

"Thank you." Rory glanced down at her clothes. "I hope you'll forgive the casual look. I was out for a run and ended up in front of your window. Your case was too good to pass up."

"Now that's what I like to hear. So what can I take out of there for you?"

Rory pointed out her choice then turned back to

Travis as Bea pulled it out for her.

"I'm actually glad I ran into you this morning. I wanted to apologize for any hard feelings after our little…discussion last night."

"You know if you really want to make it up to me you could sit with me and eat your treat. I'll even spring for coffee to go along with it."

"I'm not up to any more debating and—" she glanced down at her clothes "—I'm kind of sweaty and gross. Your friend might not want the smell competing with her baked goods."

He laughed. "That's a long way around to tell me you don't want to sit with me. Nice of you to try and make it all about you but I think I can hack the smell. I'm headed back from picking up some samples out at the bay myself, so my own aroma isn't exactly pleasant. Together we might be a threat, but I think Bea's goodies can take us."

The man had too much charm. Rory decided she'd earned a little more indulgence this morning. "In that case, make it tea and you're on."

Rory glanced around as Travis went to get their drinks. The timing was perfect as the young couple at the far table were leaving. She scooted over to snag the table, happy to finally sit down. And happy to watch Travis as he moved in and out of the other customers. He moved very well for a man so big, and the picture was one that whet her appetite for more than the scone. His ever-present grin was firmly in place as he spotted her at the table.

"I see you found us a place far enough back in the corner not to smell out Bea's customers."

He set two cups and a small basket down in front

of her. "Pick your poison."

Rory looked at the selection of herbal teas and smiled. "You brought herbal."

"My mom trained me well. I can even tell you what most of them will do to and for you."

"Is that the science part of you or the maternal training?"

He laughed. "A bit of both. Although my mom made her own herbal teas, so the training was pretty good."

She arched a brow at him. "Really?"

"Yep. She made most things like that from scratch."

"Ah, so she was Susie Homemaker." Rory thought of her own mother, whose entire life had been spent making certain her father had nothing to complain about from the time he got home until the moment he left for work again. At least not on her end.

"No, and you'd be in for a feminist lecture of epic proportions if she heard you say that." Travis chuckled. "She was Susie Earth Mother. Making things from scratch was how we connected to the land, how we respected what the earth gave us. And how we stuck it to the man by avoiding the exploitation of the industrial complex. Although that last part was more my dad's philosophy."

"Sounds very '60s."

"For them it was more the '70s but yeah, both of them were true hippies, heart and soul. That's how we ended up in Lobster Cove."

"There sounds like a story behind that."

He nodded. "A protest. They came to join the protest against the pollution of the coast. While they were here, they stumbled on Lobster Cove and fell in love, with it and with each other. They still live in the house my dad built on the other side of Grant's Lake, where all six of us kids grew up. In true hippie fashion though, they didn't marry until I was in third grade."

"Six?" Rory's eyes grew wide. "I can't imagine what it would be like with six kids in the house."

"Only child, huh?"

"Yep, the one and only issue from William and Katherine DuMont. So what persuaded them toward matrimony? You kids?"

"No. It never bothered us that they weren't married. They were happy so we were happy. It was that times had changed. Living together had gotten normal. By then everybody was doing it. People were avoiding marriage right and left. It was more common, less of a statement. So one day they woke up and decided, what the hell, they'd become legal."

Rory took another bite of the scone and a sip of the chamomile tea she'd settled on. "I have a hard time reconciling the logical scientist I met last night with that background."

He laughed. "I'll have to take you to a family dinner sometime, and you'll completely understand the reason behind my transformation. You'll also find them willing to commiserate with you over my lack of excitement over things like ghosts, along with other assorted strange beliefs they feel I should share. As to the science part, I had a biology teacher in middle school who opened my eyes to the world. He would let me come over on the weekends, ostensibly to mow his grass, but once I was done I could hang out in his library. It was filled, floor to ceiling, with books, and absolutely none of them had anything to do with anything New Age. And it was quiet. I had found my nirvana."

"A biology teacher, huh? That does explain your present condition."

"Too true. So, enough about me. Let's uncover the deeply intriguing past of our new local witch."

"You want to know more after the debate debacle?"

"I'm not looking for ghosts, just the skeletons in your closet."

"It's really obvious that you spend most of your time around pre-teens. You push the boundaries without batting an eye."

"They might not get everything right, but they do understand that if you bat your eyes you might miss something important."

"I don't know how important my life story is. Believe me, it falls more to the boring side. And I think we've probably tied up this table for long enough." She settled her cup on her now empty plate.

"Come on, I know you aren't afraid of ghosts, so what's got you nervous about letting a few skeletons out of your closet?"

Rory shook her head. "You aren't going to let up, are you?"

"Nope. But, if you're worried about freeing up Bea's table space, we could continue this conversation at dinner some time."

"Are you asking me for a date?"

"Sure am. Ned's Lobster Shack has a great special Friday nights, and if we get there by seven, we'll be sure to get a seat. We could find another table in the back, and you can tell me all about Aurora DuMont."

"I don't know. My Fridays, well...I'd have to check my calendar."

He looked at her and started to answer then his mouth turned down into a frown. "Hey, where were you?"

"What?"

Rory glared at him like he'd lost his mind before she realized his gaze wasn't on her anymore. He waved one arm over his head, and she turned to see a group of three young kids standing at the counter. The girl pretended to ignore Travis' wave by staring intently at the cookies while the other two boys gave up and walked over to their table. They looked like typical twelve-year-olds in typical Saturday morning attire to Rory, but her experience with kids was pretty limited. They wore clothes that were fashionably sloppy and had hair of varying shades of brown. Travis turned a stern stare to the tallest one.

"Where were you this morning, Justin?"

"Uh..."

The kid looked at his friend, who looked down at the floor.

"We had a deal, guys." Travis definitely had the teacher voice going. Rory figured he must be pretty effective because both boys flushed and looked apologetically at him.

"We're sorry, Mr. Reed. We...kind of got caught up in something last night and overslept this morning."

"Caught up in something? That something wouldn't be sitting out all night in the old cemetery at St. Joseph's, would it? You guys always forget that I listen when you're talking. I heard Brody talk about his plan at least five times on Friday."

Rory wouldn't have thought it possible, but their faces got redder. Her senses told her it wasn't all embarrassment either. They looked like they were about to burst with excitement as well. The girl walked over carrying a small bag and munching on a cookie with frosting Rory would swear was an inch thick. She remembered the days when she could do that with abandon and sighed.

"Did you guys tell Mr. Reed about the readings we got last night?"

The girl licked frosting from her fingers as she looked from the boys to Travis. She wore the same casual clothes as the others, but her hair was a darker black. Rory thought she teetered on the edge of teen girl blues as she noticed what might have been a smudge of eye make-up on her rich green eyes.

"Readings, huh?" Travis frowned at them. "Well, there's going to be some reading for you to do to make up for me having to go out to the shore myself and take your measurements. This ocean study is a big part of your grade, you know. You do remember your grades?"

They nodded. One of them turned to the girl and scowled.

"Thanks a lot, Amber."

She shrugged. "Well, it was cool. It could be like science, too. I mean, it's sort of like science. I mean, we made all the equipment ourselves, and last night we got some actual sound."

Rory hid her smile at the frustration on Travis' face. Amber seemed oblivious as she continued to recount their adventures.

"Although I don't think the cemetery is the best

place to hang out. I mean, that's sort of like a dead people's apartment complex, so why would their ghosts hang out there?"

"If I were a ghost, I'd go somewhere more fun than a cemetery."

The first boy had a serious look on his face that said he'd thought about this a lot. It made Rory wonder how boring the cemetery stake-out had been. "After all, everybody expects a cemetery to be haunted, and where's the fun in that?"

"My grandma's part of the Ghost Hunters, and she says where we really want to set up is in back of old Ms. DuMont's place." Rory managed not to groan as the other boy added his bit to the conversation. "Right there by the lighthouse? That's supposed to be way haunted."

"Oh, really?" Rory gave him an innocent stare.

"Uh-uh," Travis said. "You're not skating out on this that easily. Guys, this is Rory DuMont, and she knows all about ghost-hunting. She's Ms. Lorena's great-niece and the new owner of her cottage. Rory, this is Justin, Michael, and Amber."

Owning a haunted house appeared to have a great deal of appeal, for all three faces turned to her with stares of awe. Rory waved, wishing they would all stop gaping at her. Travis' face bore a shit-eating grin, and she kicked him under the table. He only grinned wider.

"Wow. You must see lots of good sh…uh, stuff."

The other two nodded at Michael's assessment. As cute as their enthusiasm for their hobby was, Rory knew it was exactly that for them, a hobby. Ghosts had played too much of a part in her own childhood for her to have that same kind of enthusiasm.

"I've seen some things." She gave them a noncommittal smile.

Amber's eyes got big, and she stared at Rory. "If we could set up there…"

"Oh, man," Justin whispered. "That's where the shipwreck ghosts are. We could really hear some sh…stuff there."

Travis glanced over at Rory with a sly smile. "Yeah, I bet you could. Ms. DuMont is very into ghosts. I bet she'd love to help you guys out."

"Could we?" Three faces turned to her with pleading eyes.

Rory thought about kicking Travis again, but then she had a better plan.

"Why not? I think a little ghost hunting sounds great. Why don't you guys come to my place this Friday, say, about seven?"

"Wow, that's awesome." The kids high-fived each other and bounced up and down.

She smiled at Travis, who shook his head.

"Trying to outmaneuver me again?"

"Not trying, did." Rory didn't even try to keep the smug look off her face.

"Not yet." Travis whistled at the kids, who had started to walk away, chattering happily. "Hey, guys, since you missed the work you were supposed to do today, why don't I join you on Friday at Ms. DuMont's. You can show me this equipment you're so proud of, and we can talk about whether or not this is science and whether or not you get credit for it."

"Yes!" Justin pumped the air and the rest of them smiled. "See you Friday. Thanks, Ms. DuMont."

"Yeah." Travis turned to her with a wicked grin.

"I'll see you Friday. Thanks, Ms. DuMont."

Chapter Three

It had been a long time since one of them woke her up from a sound sleep, Rory thought, as the ethereal presence of a young boy stared at her from the corner of her bed. Dressed in rough woolen knickers and what looked like a linen shirt, he tilted his head from side to side as if Rory were an interesting and rather foreign object. His intense stare was what had likely brought her out of sleep, for she hadn't heard him make a sound. His aura was strong, perhaps due to the fact that he was a child. According to Aunt Lorena, children have a great deal of energy to leave behind. Rory thought the boy might be around nine or ten although it was only a guess. She sighed, grateful at least that he'd wakened her in the morning rather than the middle of the night.

Aunt Lorena had taught her how to still the presence of ghost energy on one of her visits out west when Rory was thirteen. She'd been desperate to get a good night's sleep uninterrupted by her nightly visitors and had appreciated the lesson. Her father had long since given up trying to calm her nightmares, and Rory often felt her mother was more frightened than she was. She was never sure if it was the ghosts who frightened her mother or Rory herself. Aunt Lorena had shown her how to bid peace to the ghosts and encourage them on their way. She had also taught Rory some wards for her bedroom that worked to keep the energy at bay while she slept. They worked, as well, for those ghostly visitors with more malevolent natures who saw a psychic child as easy prey.

The boy appeared only to be curious without any of the chaotic bursts of energy that indicated trauma or malevolence. Early morning sun gleamed through the window, lighting the smile on his face with a translucent glow, and he raised a hand in a wave before the energy of his ghost faded away. Rory filed his image away in her mind. She would have to dig through some of Aunt Lorena's old journals to see what the boy's story was and how best to approach him. Her aunt had been meticulous with her note taking, feeling it the best way to fulfill the family job of helping the trapped spirits to move on. Rory glanced over at the alarm clock. Six a.m.

"Thanks, kid," she mumbled as she threw the covers off. "You would have to get here an hour before I had to get up." Kids, she thought. Way too full of energy living or dead.

Since she planned to spend the day scouting out businesses who might want to carry her newly produced artwork, Rory swung her legs out of bed and headed for the kitchen. Coffee might serve her better than tea this morning. The caffeine offered her the buzz she knew she needed to be able to talk to a bunch of strangers about herself.

As she strolled into the kitchen, it struck her again how comfortable she felt in this space. The night she'd arrived she had walked through the door with a bit of trepidation. Her only memory of being in *Maison de la Mer* was three weeks one summer, not long after her fifteenth birthday. Rory had begged to go when Aunt Lorena sent the invitation, and for once her mother spoke up for her. Thanks to that, her father relented and allowed Aunt Lorena to send her a ticket. It had been three of the most amazing weeks of Rory's life. Talking to someone who understood what was going on inside her had boosted her confidence and made her feel special instead of freakish.

It wasn't only Aunt Lorena that made her feel comfortable in Lobster Cove. The cottage welcomed her as well. By many people's standards, the cottage was small, with two bedrooms, a small room that Aunt Lorena referred to as the sitting room, a cozy kitchen, and a large bathroom with an antique claw foot tub. But it suited Rory perfectly. The sound of the ocean all around her made it even more perfect.

Furnished with an eye for the eclectic, *Maison de la Mer* lived up to its name. It was a home in every sense of the word. The walls were painted in soft colors that accented the contents of the room. All of the furniture was designed for comfort and beauty, a rare combination in Rory's opinion. Each piece had a history, a story behind how it came to be here and why it stayed. Aunt Lorena was a collector, and she'd traveled all over the world. Her home was a reflection of all she was. Being here had strengthened Rory's resolve to follow in her aunt's footsteps. Here, in Lobster Cove, in the place created by a woman she had loved and who had returned that love, Rory could be herself. As she sat down with her coffee and opened the folder of designs she hoped would open up a new life for her, she sent her aunt a prayer of thanks for her gift.

An hour later, dressed in the silky, red tunic top,

boots, and black leggings that she thought made her look artsy, Rory stood before the heavy wood door of The Shucker's Booktique. In her hands she clutched the black folder that held her plans for a new future. She'd worked all week on the portfolio for this visit and, thanks to her early morning visitor, had enough time this morning to polish it up a bit more.

The idea of running her own graphic arts business had been a cherished dream for a long time. Making that dream into a reality turned out to be a scarier proposition than she'd imagined. Selling herself hadn't been part of the dream version, so the realization that she would have to do exactly that to get her foot in the door had hit her like a splash of cold ocean water.

She'd picked The Shucker's Booktique as her first conquest because of the feeling it gave off as she stood in front of the window. And because she had gotten a really nice shot of the yard that had yielded a great little notecard set.

Both old and new, modern and ancient, the vibrations she got from the building were good ones, and Rory had learned to go with her intuition on things like this. Listening to her inner voice usually turned out for the best. Usually. It had failed her where Travis Reed was concerned. No matter how much she enjoyed bantering with him, her instincts told her a relationship would be the same disastrous train wreck that the others had been. She'd spent too many of those relationships trying to live up, or in a couple of cases down, to their expectations. Being herself had spelled the end of each one. When she came to Lobster Cove it was with the promise that she would live the way she wanted to live, be who she truly was. If that meant she lived a sexless, relationship-less existence while she was here, then she'd suck it up and deal with that. After all, the plan was only to stay for six months. *Surely she could be celibate for six months, couldn't she?* Don't answer that, she told her inner voice just as it started to chime in. *It was a rhetorical question.* She was thirty years old, and she owed it to herself to finally start being who she was inside. Her crazed hormonal attraction to Travis Reed was not going to interfere with the plan.

Rory had been certain she'd forestalled any date nights with her clever turn of inviting his students to her house. Her cleverness had backfired, and now she had to figure out how to keep three young kids from stirring up anymore ghost energy in her house and how to keep Travis Reed from stirring up any more sexual energy in her body. Friday was going to be a busy day. With her thoughts rambling around like wild cards, Rory struggled to focus as she pushed open the door and walked in.

It was like walking into heaven. She was a historical nut, which was why the job in Denver had suited her so well. Spending her days viewing old photographs and artifacts was sheer nirvana. Turning them into exciting exhibits had come easily, and she had to admit she missed it. Standing inside the huge old home which had been cleverly converted to a veritable smorgasbord of books, prints and assorted small items of a rather eclectic nature, Rory felt like she'd come home.

The room smelled of the years and history held within its walls. Classical music echoed softly in the space, adding an extra lure to the potential customers who entered. It was set up with a good eye for marketing, something that Rory knew would be important to where she placed her products. There was no point in selling herself if the buyer couldn't then sell her work. From the looks of The Booktique, the owner here knew how to run a successful business.

She hadn't stood there long when a man wandered in from the back, another plus sign for a good business. Greeting customers was important. This man would be a welcome greeter, too. He was handsome, well over six feet tall, with dark black hair and porcelain white skin. The combination made him seem rather otherworldly. Something about him nagged at her, but she pushed it aside. Her presentation needed to come off focused and professional. This meeting was about business, about her future.

Rory smiled as she started toward him, her practiced speech prepared. Then she stopped as a cold wave of energy hit her. Wave was a good word for what hit her, Rory thought, as the feel of a roiling ocean wave rushed over her. Her gaze caught the man's face and the intensity of the feeling deepened.

He wore a cautious look as he took in her appearance, scrutinizing her from head to toe in a way that screamed suspicion. Her confidence sank at the thought of the gossip centered on her. Hoping to find out how best to approach the situation, Rory sneaked a peek at his aura, not surprised to find it matched the stormy feeling hitting her, the swirls of gray, blue and white all around him making her feel as if she were on a boat being tossed about on the sea. For a moment they stood staring at each other, as if each of them were taking the measure of the other. Rory cleared her throat and picked up the pieces of her confidence.

"Hello."

"Hello." The man nodded, his expression still wary but his voice friendly.

At least they were making progress, Rory thought. "My name is Aurora DuMont. I've just moved to Lobster Cove and I wanted to—"

"Lorena DuMont's niece?"

"Yes." Rory smiled bigger. "Yes, she was my aunt. She's actually the reason I moved here. I'm living in her cottage out by the lighthouse."

"Yes, I'd heard that."

"Um, did you know my aunt?"

"Yes." He didn't seem inclined to carry any more of the weight of the conversation than he had to.

"Oh, well. Good." Rory took a deep breath. This wasn't going to get any better if they just kept staring at each other so she might as well plunge ahead. "I was hoping to talk with—"

"Lon, did someone come…oh, hello."

A pretty young woman came in from the back, wiping her hands on a towel. She smiled at Rory before turning a quick frown on the man beside her. The two of them made an interesting pair, the tiny woman barely coming up to the man's chest. She was pretty, with wavy chestnut brown hair and friendly eyes. A look passed between them then the woman stuck out her hand.

"Hello. I'm Willa, Willa Devlin."

"Rory. Rory DuMont. Hi."

Relief washed over Rory at the friendly smile in the woman's amber eyes. "I was telling this gentleman here that I have just moved to Lobster Cove."

"You're Lorena's niece."

"Yes," Rory said, hoping the conversation didn't go downhill again. "Yes, I'm living in her cottage now, and I wanted to come by and speak with the owner of this beautiful bookstore."

"That would be us." She waved a hand at the man. "This is Lon, my husband."

Rory stuck out a hand to him, and he took it. As they touched she felt that peculiar energy wave again. When he released her hand, he smiled at her. Rory wondered what information she had passed to him through that quick touch. Whatever it was, he seemed more relaxed with her presence than he had before.

Willa motioned her to two chairs set in a cozy corner of the store. As they settled into them, she turned to Rory with the same friendly smile.

"Now what can I do for you?"

****

An hour later Rory walked back through her door without her black portfolio and with a bag from Sweet Bea's. Her portfolio was now part of Willa's inventory, and the slice of vanilla cake with raspberry filling in the bag was her reward. She wanted to pump her fist in the air as Travis' kids had done. The whole conversation had gone better than she could have ever hoped. Willa had loved her designs and was excited about adding Rory's products to her inventory. The thought of her pretty notecards and prints on the shelves of the bookstore made her happier than she'd thought possible. Now she could accept that she really was an artist. It was her eye and her imagination that created the products. She had sold herself, and it felt really good. Now for that vanilla cake with raspberry filling.

As she walked into the kitchen, she glanced out the

window, wanting to send a thank you to the water spirits who had been so helpful in guiding her to some of the best spots for her pictures. Staring out at the water, she noticed a lone figure crouched in the rocks below. People sometimes walked along the shoreline behind the cottage, so at first, she didn't give her visitor much thought. But as she opened the window to let in some fresh air, she heard the moaning. Whoever it was below was crying, deep horrible sobs that echoed off the crashing waves.

Rory stepped out the back door, thinking she would at least go and check on the person. She'd only gotten a few steps down the steep hillside when the pain hit her, and she couldn't stifle the moan. Wave after wave of the deepest agony rolled over her as it radiated off the woman standing on the rocks. The pain felt endless. Rory sank to her knees under the weight of it. She breathed in and out slowly, working through the assault as she let her gaze wander out along the shoreline. The sound of her own moans must have carried out to the water for the woman turned her gaze toward the cottage.

Rory let out a gasp as she saw her visitor was Margaret Vincent. For a moment their eyes met, and Rory saw sadness deeper than any she'd ever known shining out of Margaret's tear-filled eyes. Margaret quickly masked the emotion with a glare in Rory's direction. Before Rory could move, Margaret turned and scrambled back up the rocks and headed down the road.

It took Rory a minute to collect herself. When she felt her legs could hold her again, she rose and carefully picked her way down to the shoreline. She wanted to walk by the water and send some healing energy out to the sprites and the water itself. The psychic residue of the kind of pain Margaret had been radiating would be a tremendous burden for the elementals. As she walked along she recited the simple cleansing ritual she'd written when she was a teenager. It had served her well for years, and she felt the last of the residue leave her own spirit as the words flowed out of her.

Her gaze wandered along the shoreline as she let the sound of the waves wash away the last of Margaret's pain. When she looked out toward the lighthouse, she almost let out another gasp. Travis stood among the rocks, his feet half in the water. He was shirtless, the sun glinting off the fire of his hair making him look like a true Viking warrior out for conquest, with his gaze focused out on the rolling waves. Rory's mouth watered at the sight of him, and moisture gathered in other places as well. The picture he made standing there reminded her of one of those romance covers she'd seen in The Shucker's Booktique. There was a whole line of them by a lady named Scarlette LaFlamme, and the covers were those they used to call bodice-rippers. Rory had never understood the term until now. As she stared at Travis standing there by the ocean looking like a barbarian conqueror come to claim his kingdom she thought, hell, I'd rip my own bodice off at a sight like that, along with whatever was left of his clothes. When he bent over to pick up something from the water, the sight of all those muscles rippling along his broad shoulders had Rory letting out a sigh.

His jeans rode low on his hips as he reached over to pick the small vials out of the water, and Rory found herself wishing they would dip just a bit lower. Or maybe a lot lower. The rich tan of his back extended down to the waist of his jeans, and she wondered how far it went. There was some exploring she could get into, she thought, even as her inner voice encouraged her to walk away, just walk away. But today was a day for indulgence, so she ignored the warning and walked toward him instead.

Travis must have heard her approach, for he turned as she drew near. When he saw her, he watched appreciatively as she made her way to his spot, and Rory felt grateful she didn't have a bodice on cause she was sure she'd have ripped it right then. Still, it felt good to have a man look at her like that, like she was a meal and he was more than hungry. Then and there Rory decided that appreciation was a nice quality in a man.

"We've got to stop meeting like this." He grinned at her as he said it. "People are going to talk, you know."

She arched a brow at him. "According to you, I'm already the talk of the town. Besides, you're kind of in my backyard."

"True." He gazed out at the water lapping against the shoreline. "Although I'm not sure yard is the right term."

"People would probably object if I called it my ocean. And my pile of rocks just doesn't have the same ring to it."

"You've got me there. Whatever you call it, it's beautiful. I love the fall the best." He bent over to pick up the rest of his containers, reaching for his shirt as well. She thought he might have seen the hint of disappointment in her eyes, for there was a bit of a twinkle in his as he pulled it over his head. He offered her a hand as they headed back up the rocks.

"So, Ms. DuMont, are you stalking me?"

"I'm offended, Mr. Reed. I'll have you know I majored in Stalking 101 back in high school. And I aced the class. If I were stalking you, it would never be this obvious."

"Good to know. I'll have to start keeping a sharper eye on things going on around me then."

"You'll never see me."

"That's okay. I'm seeing you now, and it's a welcome sight."

"Flattery will get you nowhere, Reed. I'm a tougher nut than that to crack."

"So what kind of charm would it take to get me an offer of a bathroom to use to wash up a bit?"

She looked over at him with a wicked smile. "Magic words. Does a scientist know any magic words?"

"No magic words. We deal in formulas, and that's a pretty common one. At least for any kid who had a mother like mine." He took her hand to help her over the rocks, and Rory felt that hot tingle of energy again. This time it aimed for parts of her that were already pretty heated up. With a grin to match her own, Travis gave her a little bow.

"Ms. DuMont, may I please have the use of your facilities? Your generosity would be much appreciated as I smell sort of like the ocean, but in its much less clean and crisp stages."

"I don't know about magical, but those words conjure up the need to follow your visit to my bathroom with a thorough cleaning."

He laughed. "You provide the rag and the cleaner, and I'll provide the rest."

They made their way up the slope and back to the cottage. Rory was struck by how easy it felt to walk along beside him. He set all her bells ringing in a freakishly sexual manner, but he also made her feel comfortable, a side effect that made no sense. Travis was fun, sure, but he was also sensible, logical and thoughtful. None of those were traits that had ever been applied to her. Maybe her mother was right when she said Rory spent too much time questioning things and not enough time just letting them be. After all, wasn't that what she had come to Lobster Cove for, to learn to be herself and let go of struggling to be something she wasn't?

When they walked in the door, Travis sighed. She frowned over at him, but there was a big smile on his face as he looked around the room.

"Ah, I haven't been in here in years. From the looks of things, nothing's changed." He glanced over at her. "My mom used to bring Ms. Lorena some of her teas. I tagged along most of the time because it meant I got to play by the ocean."

Rory nodded. "That was what attracted Aunt Lorena to the cottage. She loved the sound of the ocean at night. It was always a kind of magical place for me. I never spent much time here as a kid. Aunt Lorena usually came to see us. My father wasn't about to give up any of his vacation time to come all the way to Maine to see a woman he thought was a blight on the family name, so we never traveled to Maine to return the favor. When I got older, it seemed like I came when I needed a place to hide. Or to heal. It was good for that."

"There was a good woman who lived here. That's what helped most I bet."

Rory looked over at him thoughtfully. "You're right, although it makes me wonder how you know that. I can't imagine you coming out very well arguing with Aunt Lorena about ghosts." She nodded toward the hall. "I guess you know where the bathroom is if you've been in here before."

He put his containers down by the door before entering. "Your aunt was a woman of many interests. And you're right; I would never have dared debate her on the ghost topic." He took the towel Rory handed him. "I mentioned it one time as a very young, smart-ass kid, and she took my argument apart in thirty seconds. We learned to agree to disagree after a time."

"Now that sounds more like Aunt Lorena. She always said it was best to let people find out things on their own. When they disagreed with her, she never doubted that if they really looked into things they would come around to her side of it."

"Confidence is an attractive trait in a woman."

He headed toward the bathroom, the towel thrown over one shoulder.

Rory snorted. "You're a rare man to think so."

Travis stopped and turned back to her. There was no grin on his face this time. "It is one of the most attractive traits a woman can have."

His tone was dead serious, and for a moment Rory just stared at him. Then his face split into a grin as he pulled the towel off his shoulder.

"But you're right, I am a rare man."

With that pronouncement, he strode out of the

room.

"That you are, Travis Reed," Rory murmured. "That you are."

Chapter Four

"All cleaned up."

Rory looked up as Travis came into the kitchen. She sniffed at him.

"Well, the ocean aroma is gone. Can't say that's a bad thing."

"Your bathroom and I are both ready for company."

"Pull up a chair and I'll get you a cup. You can celebrate with me."

"What are we celebrating? Whoa!" Travis gave a whistle as Rory placed the vanilla cake on the table in front of him. "Whatever it is, it must be important. That's Bea's vanilla cake."

"With raspberry filling."

"Yep, that's it. So what happened to the woman whose standards only included making the logical choice for good nutrition?"

"She did something amazing today." It felt good to say it out loud. "And now she's celebrating. Or rather we're celebrating." She handed Travis a plate and a fork, then sliced the cake in two.

"A celebration? Now that I can get into. So exactly what amazing thing did you do today?"

"I sold myself."

"Okay, not quite what I was expecting."

She laughed. "Me either. I was expecting to fall flat

on my face, to end up sounding like a stammering fool and getting tossed out on my ass."

"Since we're celebrating, I take it things didn't go that way."

"No, they didn't. As a matter of fact, they went the completely opposite direction from that scenario. And soon you, and everyone else in Lobster Cove, will be able to see the evidence of how well it went today."

"So there's evidence, hmm?"

"Well, it hasn't happened yet, but should you by some chance wander into The Shucker's Booktique three weeks from now, you will be enchanted by the beautiful prints for sale there. Prints by Lobster Cove's newest local artist."

"Then I will have to make sure I wander in there three weeks from now. And my congratulations to our newest local artist. Willa has a good eye and a good head for business. She and Lon have done wonders with the place. Having your work there should be a plus when it comes to your sales."

"I certainly hope so. She seemed to know her business, and she plans on giving me some prime space on the endcaps. I was excited, once I got past the nerves."

"Nerves?"

"I've spent the last eight years hiding away in a tiny back room, chained to my computer. People saw my work all the time but didn't even know I existed. It wasn't easy to walk in there cold and sell myself."

"But you did it. You succeeded. And now you have cake."

Rory lifted a fork in a salute. "And now I have cake." She sighed as she swallowed the bite. "Luscious, sinfully delicious cake."

"That's the best kind." He gave her a look of sheer innocence. "Things that are sinfully delicious should be part of your life more often if one bite puts that kind of look on your face."

"I don't run enough to burn off the calories from indulging any more often than I do."

"I know a few things that fall into the category of sinfully delicious that wouldn't add any extra calories at all. As a matter of fact, the activities I'm thinking of burn off calories. You can trust me on that. I'm a scientist."

"Is that so?"

"Yes, it is. I can come over and show you sometime if you'd like."

Rory looked him up and down. "Now that's an offer I'm going to have to give some serious thought to." She grinned at him. "But you're already coming back over here on Friday. Maybe we could do a demo then."

"With an audience of snotty kids standing around to critique me? Not hardly."

"What, a confident man like you? I can't see why an audience would scare you off."

"Got nothing to do with confidence or being scared off. It's that having an audience of pre-teen punks wouldn't give the moment the ambiance it needs." Travis winked at her. "When I get the chance to show you're what you're missing, Ms. DuMont, it's going to be the right place at the right time." He rose and took his plate to the sink. "And you think you're the talk of the town now. It'll be nothing compared to the rumors those little heathens would spread."

He walked back to the table, and Rory swore the temperature around her went up ten degrees.

"Well, um, it sounds like your demo is pretty personal." Rory was surprised she could get the words out at all with the images his words created all tangled up in her brain.

"Yeah, it is." The amusement was gone from his voice, replaced by a tone far more sensual. "Up close and personal."

She had been watching his face, which was the only excuse she could find for not noticing his hands move. Before she knew it, Travis had pulled her up from her chair and put his mouth on hers. The kiss took the breath right out of her, and the feel of that muscled chest against her breasts took the resistance right out of her. Any thought she had about stepping back fled as she wrapped her arms around his neck. It was all the response he needed. His tongue swept past her lips as he pulled her tight against him. She could taste the sweetness of the cake and the maleness of him as he claimed her mouth. It was a heady combination. Rory thought she might have moaned but it was too hard to hear anything over the roar in her ears. All too soon he pulled back, leaving the taste of him on her lips and a longing for more deep inside her. She steadied herself with a hand against the table.

"I think you're right. That's probably something we should skip while your students are here."

"Another time, then."

She stared at him for a moment, then she licked her lips. A slow smile spread across his face as she did.

"Um, as good as that…demo was, I don't know if another time is a good idea. I feel it only fair to warn you that the whole dating, romance, sex thing…"

"Yeah?"

"I'm not really good at that."

"Oh? What part aren't you good at 'cause I'm not seeing a problem so far?"

"I'm not good at any of it. Things start off okay but somewhere around let's-have-some-fun and it's-time-to-get-serious, my romance train derails. Sometimes it's even been known to crash and burn. There are no survivors when it does."

She kept her eyes off his face as she gathered up the plates and forks. No sense staring at what she was giving up.

"No survivors, huh?"

"Yeah." She paused. "The whole relationship suffers a fatality. It's not a pretty sight."

"Maybe you've just never gotten on the right train. Maybe your destination's been wrong all those other times."

She shook her head. "I don't know. I think—"

"Rory." Travis moved up behind her, turning her to face him. "I'm really good at what I do."

She gave him a confused look, and he laughed.

"Well, I'm good at that, too, but what I meant was I'm a good teacher. I believe in giving the learning process time."

"Oh. Well. Time is always a good thing." Rory edged past him to take the dishes to the sink. Brushing up against him didn't do wonders for her rattled hormones. "I guess if you want to take the time…"

"I do."

Boy didn't those words sound dangerous. Rory decided it was time to get off this path and onto a safer one.

"Um, speaking of your students—"

"Is that what we were doing?" Amusement bled back into his tone.

"I'm sure they were mixed in there somewhere."

She turned to face him, hoping her cheeks weren't as flushed as they felt. "I was wondering about Friday. I thought I'd fix some food, maybe try out some of the recipes Jane gave me, but in case you haven't guessed, I don't really know a whole lot about kids. They may not like their food too…complicated. What do you feed eleven-year-old boys?"

"Food and lots of it."

"That sounds simple."

"It is. A lot of things are simple, Rory, if you let them be."

Where had she heard that before, she thought.

****

Rory decided to take Travis' advice, at least where the kids were concerned. Simple turned out to be burgers and corn on the cob. It was more generic American than any of the Maine specialty recipes Jane had given her. Those she would save for another time. The kids loved it and consumed the food as if starving. She didn't know if that should give her confidence a boost or teach her to prepare more next time.

All of them, including Travis, had arrived at seven on the dot. They'd carpooled in Travis' truck. He had promised their parents to have them back by ten, no matter how successful the hunting. After moaning at the thought of interrupting what they were certain would be a productive evening, the kids unloaded the truck and went about setting up their "equipment." In spite of

Travis' snorts when they unpacked the items they'd brought with them and showed them off, they set about staging the scene with a seriousness worthy of any scientist. Even Travis gave them credit for researching the items and learning how to create their own equipment, albeit grudgingly.

All of the kids wanted to set up in Rory's bedroom, but she'd nixed that plan. They were too polite to complain after she'd refused their pleas, so with looks that told her they felt their hunt would be far less successful thanks to her, the kids compromised and decided to set up their equipment in the sitting room. Memories of the Ghost Hunters Society flitted through her mind as Rory watched the miniature versions of the adults she'd seen at the meeting display the same excitement and anticipation over the potential presence of a ghostly entity. Their standards didn't sound too high, either. The thought of getting even a sound or a light on what Justin referred to as their full-spectrum camera seemed to be enough to satisfy them. Rory had to stifle more than one giggle as Justin and Michael argued with Amber over proper placement of the camera and the best location for what they called a "spirit box," which looked to Rory like an old AM/FM radio. Michael explained to her with total seriousness that he and his dad had spent last evening modifying the old radio, and it would emit any frequencies the ghosts chose to use. They were so dedicated that Rory didn't have the heart to tell them the ghost of the young boy she'd seen earlier watched them the whole time they were setting up. He looked as interested as his living counterparts. This was going to be a long evening.

Travis helped her with the dishes as the kids

finished their argument over equipment. He glanced at them one more time then rolled his eyes as he handed her another plate.

"Come on." Rory laughed. "You've got to give them an "A" now, even if just for the effort."

"Don't encourage them."

"If you can't beat 'em, join 'em. That's always been my motto."

"Not a good teaching technique. There are standards to meet, you know."

"You're out of school, Teach. Relax and enjoy it."

He grinned down at her. "Now there's a plan I could get behind."

Rory stepped away from him to put a plate away. "No demo tonight, remember."

"There are other ways to relax, my dear." He gave her a leer as he raised an eyebrow.

"A look like that doesn't make me relax."

"Hey, we got it all set up." Amber poked her head into the kitchen. "Want to come see?"

"Guess we'll have to continue this another time." Rory handed Travis a towel to dry his hands.

"You do know that this *another time* you keep putting things off to is going to come someday, don't you?"

And Goddess willing I'll be ready for it, thought Rory as she ignored his comment to follow Amber out to the sitting room.

The kids had turned off all the lights, and she and Travis were handed goggles as they came into the sitting room to, as Michael explained it, protect their eyes from any ghost flashes. Though she'd feared the time would drag, the evening went faster than Rory expected. Justin and Michael were hilarious as they jumped to adjust their equipment at every noise and spot that could be seen on their camera.

It was hard to keep the giggles quiet as she watched them, but she and Travis had been carefully instructed in the protocol of ghost hunting. Noise was unacceptable. Travis earned more than his share of frowns for the occasional comments he couldn't resist as they discussed what was happening in furtive whispers that had him rolling his eyes. Sitting beside him, Rory found herself grateful for the silence. It allowed her to enjoy looking at him and listening to his banter with the kids without the worry of her own inability to make conversation with them. He had an easy way with them that they seemed to respond too in spite of his clear disapproval of what they were doing. Genuine affection laced his teasing, and they took it as such. In spite of his own distaste for ghost hunting, he also encouraged them to think about the scientific method in their observations. At one point, he really seemed to get into the whole experiment. That was after there had been a strong reading on both the camera and the little spirit box. They had all, Travis included, grouped around the equipment to whisper about the meaning of the readings. As they did, Rory looked up to see the wavering ether of an older woman standing across the room with a disapproving look on her face. Seems their ghost didn't approve of being hunted, she thought with a smile before turning back to listen to their chatter.

"We should compare this to the flash from the cemetery."

Amber sounded quite business-like as she

instructed the boys on how to record the time in their little log.

"Good records are important." Travis nodded. "Very scientific," he added, tongue firmly in cheek.

Finally nine-thirty rolled around. Rory hated to break up the party, but she knew it would take them a bit to round up all the equipment.

"Guys," she interrupted. "Time to pack it up."

"Aww." Three faces turned to her with disappointing frowns.

"Sorry, but she's right." Travis stood and stretched. "Your parents will be waiting back at the school. Let's get all this packed up. And by us, I mean you guys."

They rolled their eyes but started to shut everything down, carefully storing their equipment back in the bags. Rory walked around the room picking up cups and leftover granola bar wrappers. In spite of consuming everything she'd had for dinner, the kids had apparently decided more nutrition was needed. Ghost hunting was apparently a strenuous activity. They had brought their own snacks. Rory wondered if it had been in case they hadn't liked her dinner, but Travis informed her the trio never went anywhere without food of some sort.

"Here." Travis took the trash from her hand. "Let me help you with that."

She glanced around the room. The ghost had left over an hour ago, leaving behind a few flashes and what the kids thought was a moan, but Rory was certain a laugh erupted out of the old woman.

"Well, that was fun." She grinned up at Travis as she walked with him to the kitchen.

Travis groaned. "They won't stop talking about it

for a week. Every little flash, every tiny sound is going to have come straight from a ghost as far as they're concerned. I'll never get them talked out of it now."

"Would it help if I told you there were ghosts in the room?"

He snorted. "You're just messing with me now."

Rory gave him an innocent stare, and he frowned. "Aren't you?"

She wanted to laugh at the consternation on his face. "Yes." The answer came out of her mouth too easily, and she thought about her promise to herself. "No."

"Yes and no?"

Rory blew out a breath. "If I tell you yes, I'm messing with you when I say there were ghosts here tonight then you're okay with that. You're comfortable with it. If I tell you no, that there really was a ghost, two in fact, here tonight, then the train derails and you run for the hills."

He stared at her for a moment with a thoughtful look on his face. "Tell me what you believe you saw."

"The truth?"

Travis nodded. "The truth of what you believe you saw."

"That's a very guarded way of putting it."

"No. It's a very scientific way of putting it. I can't know what to think if I don't have all the evidence."

"Fair enough. I saw two ghosts."

"Whole images?"

"One fairly solid, a little boy and one kind of wavering, an older woman."

He watched her face as she said it, and Rory held her breath, waiting for the sneer that had always

53

accompanied any talk of her gift in the past. She would be sorry to see him walk away. Even though it had only been a few weeks, she realized she'd come to enjoy his company. Part of her knew she'd been hoping for something more, no matter how much she told herself she wasn't going to do another relationship. Still, it would hurt, and she steeled herself for the good-bye. At last he nodded.

"Okay, you saw two ghosts."

"You're not headed for the door."

"The kids aren't packed up yet." He grinned. "And the train is still on the tracks, Ms. DuMont. Nothing's derailed yet."

"Willing to take a chance on a crazy lady, is that it?"

Rory found she didn't like the words even as she said them. Something about the idea that he would stick around to find out how crazy she was didn't feel any better than the idea he would walk away because he thought her crazy.

He stepped up to her, and before she could blink, he'd planted a hard kiss on her lips. As he moved back, she could only stare at him, not certain what to say or if she should say anything at all. He shook his head.

"Willing to take the time to find out about a beautiful and very interesting lady that I've become attracted to."

"Wow. That makes me sound worth the effort."

"Because you are. And I believe if you spend some time with me, you'll find I am worth the effort, too. I believe in the scientific method, Rory."

"Was that what that kiss was?"

He smiled. "Not exactly. What it was was me

investigating. See, that's how it works. I put out my hypothesis, and then I look at all the evidence."

"Including the fact that I see ghosts."

"Including the fact that you *think* you see ghosts."

Rory rolled her eyes. "So what comes after I tell you I see ghosts?"

"Then I explore the evidence. We explore it together. We can start our experiment by you coming with me to the Harvest of the Sea."

"The festival in town?"

"Yep. It's downtown, a week from tomorrow so I'll have time to persuade you. You'll love it. I can pick you up that Saturday at ten."

"I don't know…"

"You'll be advancing the cause of science. That's the best way to uncover the truth of my hypothesis. I have to find out all the evidence, go beyond the surface. That's how science works. I'll probably have to do some other experiments, too."

"Other experiments?

"Yeah. Kind of check things out in a more private setting, get some personal responses for my notes."

"Personal responses? What kind of responses?"

"Well, let's see."

This time she knew the kiss was coming, but it didn't change any of her response. The moment his lips touched hers, she felt the room spin, and everything inside her heat up. She decided then and there Travis was really good at this. Better than good. He pushed the kiss past the limits of attraction and into the realm of hot enough to burn. Rory thought she might be having an out-of-body experience until she heard a loud gagging noise.

"Eww!"

She looked over at the door to find all three kids staring at them. Justin and Michael looked horrified, and Amber looked mad. A bit of a crush, Rory thought. Travis hadn't looked over. He just leaned his forehead on hers. She felt his shoulders shaking and realized he was laughing.

"I think your experiment just got contaminated," she whispered.

He looked up at her with a twinkle in his eye. "No, not completely. The data is good but incomplete. We'll have to try this again another time, you know. You can't stop things now. Think of the blow to the scientific community."

Rory smacked him on the shoulder as she hissed at him. "They're listening!"

He laughed. "Okay, guys, I take it you got all the stuff packed up."

"Uh, yeah." Justin looked from him to Rory and back. "Yeah. We're ready to go. Thanks for everything, Ms. DuMont."

"You're welcome, Justin." Rory looked over at Travis. "Looks like science class is over for tonight."

"Nuh-uh. It's only recess." Travis winked at her before he turned to the three in the doorway. "Okay, guys, into the truck."

As they waved goodbye to Rory and headed out the door, Travis turned back to her. "Class isn't over by a longshot. Keep that in mind, Ms. DuMont."

She was going to have a lot on her mind until the bell rang again, Rory thought. A whole lot.

Chapter Five

"Perfect fit." Travis adjusted the cap on Rory's head. "And the perfect souvenir of your first Harvest of the Sea festival."

Rory reached up and tugged at her new lobster-red headgear. The claws hung out over her forehead, and the floppy tail at the end bopped up and down against her neck.

"I don't think it's the look I'm going for."

"Oh, sure it is. You're a hit already. Just look at everybody staring at you."

Rory groaned. "You mean just look at everybody pointing and laughing."

"Maine folk are too polite to laugh to your face. They'll save it up for when they get home."

"I'm trying to fit in here, not remain the talk of the town."

Travis took her hand as they headed down the pier. "Honey, you'll be the talk of the town until someone else new moves in. That's the way gossip works. Talk will die down when a better topic comes along. Unless you provide that better topic, you should be okay in a few years."

"It's always so encouraging to talk to you about things."

He smiled. "Always happy to make you feel better. Now aren't you glad I encouraged you to come with me today?"

"I'm not sure encouraged is the right word. There's got to be one that fits better, say, oh, let me think...blackmailed, browbeat...badgered..."

"I simply reminded you we needed to finish our experiment. The cause of science is ever at the forefront of my mind."

"Uh-huh. I thought scientists valued accurate observation. You and I must have been observing a very different conversation if you think *reminded* even comes close to the way you got me out here today."

Though she didn't plan on letting Travis off the hook that easily, Rory had to admit the day had been more fun than she expected. She had spent all last week working on new designs and getting inventory printed up to take to The Shucker's Booktique. Willa had offered to have a reception to showcase her work at the store. It was a wonderful offer, but it also left Rory with a serious case of butterflies in her stomach.

When Travis called, she'd thought to put him off. Her plan had been to polish the new work a bit more. The Harvest of the Sea festival, an annual October event in Lobster Cove, had sounded a bit like a school carnival when he mentioned it. He reminded her it was Saturday, and that it could be an opportunity for some new shots. Rory had brought her camera and had gotten a few photos but mostly she had played. The day had been a blast, and she was glad she'd accepted Travis' invitation, in spite of the lobster hat now balanced on her head. And in spite of the copious amounts of food she'd inhaled since arriving in town. Many of the local restaurants had set up booths to sell samples of their specialties. Rory had tried lobster rolls, clam and lobster chowder, and even a lobster-shaped cookie. It had all been delicious.

"You're grateful I dragged you out of the house, and you know it."

"I'm not going to be grateful when I can't fit into any of my clothes anymore."

"You know, I could think of a few activities that wouldn't require you to wear any clothes. If things don't fit after today you wouldn't have to worry about it."

"Haha. I don't think I would ever stop being the talk of the town if I decided to stroll around Lobster Cove skyclad."

"True, but—" he looked her up and down with a mock leer "—the gossip would be very favorable."

Rory rolled her eyes. "Just steer me away from anymore food booths, and I think I'll be okay."

"If you insist. Course, Sweet Bea's should have a booth out here somewhere, too. We haven't passed it yet."

Rory groaned. "We aren't going to either. I can't hold another thing. If I'd have known there was going to be this much food here, I'd have insisted we walk into town."

"Then how could we have carried all your important stuff home?" Travis pointed at the bag in his hand. Sticking out of the top was a huge stuffed lobster wearing a stupid grin and a pair of sunglasses.

"What is it with putting sunglasses on lobsters?" Rory mused. "I don't get the connection."

"The connection is the company that makes the lobsters also makes the sunglasses."

"Ah, I see."

"Two birds, one stone."

"Hey, Ms. Dumont, Mr. Reed."

Coming down the pier toward them were Justin, Michael, and Amber. The Paranormal Posse, as Travis had dubbed them, had clearly made the rounds of the food vendors, although from the looks of their faces and the assorted wrappings in their hands, their choices had steered more to the sweet side than the seafood one. Michael was still munching on a lobster-shaped cookie.

"Hi guys." Travis waved them over. "Checking out the vendors, I see."

"We've been putting together the stuff we got at your house, Ms. DuMont." Justin seemed very excited so Rory gave him her best listening look. "It's awesome, the best we've ever gotten. We thought we could...well, we hoped that...."

"Can we do it again?"

Justin frowned at Amber for the interruption. "That's sort of what I was getting to."

"Slowly." Amber rolled her eyes at him. "Geez, she doesn't want to stand here all day."

Michael shook his head at both of them. "Well, Ms. DuMont, could we?"

"Could you...?" Rory looked from the eager young faces to Travis.

"I think they're trying to ask if you would let them come back to your house for another night of ghost-hunting."

"Umm..."

"Please?"

Rory could tell the trio was torn between looking cool and pleading. It would take a harder heart than hers to disappoint them, she thought. Giving up another

Friday night didn't seem like such a bad thing, she guessed. Then she had an idea.

"I suppose we could arrange something. But I have a little different idea in mind than the set-up you had before."

"Different?"

She could tell she had their attention now. Travis' too. He was giving her a look that told her he wondered what she was up to. Chances were if she extended the invitation she had in mind to him as well, it just might send their romance train off the tracks after all. But what the hell, she thought. If it was going to happen better to get it done and over with before she headed back out west.

"A bit different. But you'd have to have your parents' permission to come."

"Okay, sure." They all shrugged as if it were no problem.

"Don't be too quick. What I'm inviting you to is a Dumb Supper."

Travis raised a brow, but the kids just looked confused. Amber looked at her as if she wanted to say something but wasn't sure she should. Finally she leaned over to Travis and whispered.

"Should she really be saying something like that, Mr. Reed? I mean, I can't ask my mom to go to a dumb supper. She's going to think I'm being mean, and I'll get in trouble."

Travis struggled to hide the grin. "It's okay, Amber. It's an old-fashioned term, and at the time it was used, it simply meant someone who didn't speak."

"Didn't speak? Cause they were dumb?" Michael stared at her.

"Still doesn't sound nice." Amber folded her arms over her chest and glared at Rory.

Rory held up her hands. "I mean no offense, Amber. A Dumb Supper is an old tradition in my religion. You know what holiday it is in a couple of weeks, right?"

"Sure."

They all nodded.

"It's Halloween."

Justin looked at the other two as if to say, well, duh.

Rory nodded. "Yes, it's Halloween, or All Hallows Eve, which is an old name for it."

"Like Harry Potter, huh?" Michael smiled as if he finally understood the conversation. "Like the Deathly Hallows."

This time Travis didn't keep the grin off his face. He appeared to be having way too much fun watching Rory try to explain what she meant to the kids. Probably he was just enjoying watching someone else do what he did five days a week, she thought.

"Well, sort of. There's another name for Halloween, an even older name that's used in my religion. It's Samhain."

"Your religion celebrates Halloween? Cool."

Rory could tell she had just gone way up in Michael's estimation at least. The jury was still out on Justin and Amber. Justin looked confused, and Amber was still frowning at her like she'd said a bad word.

"Yes, we celebrate Halloween, but we do it in a little different way. When Wiccans celebrate Samhain, some of us hold what's called a Dumb Supper. It's a meal where everyone there is given a plate of food, even those people who are only there in spirit."

"You mean as ghosts? It's a ghost supper?" Amber looked like she didn't believe her.

Rory laughed. "Sort of. Wiccans believe that the veil between this world, the world of the living, and the next world, the world people go to when they die, is thinner at Samhain than at other times of the year. What that means to us is that those we love who have passed on through that veil, those who have died, can communicate with us more easily at Samhain than at other times of the year. So we set a place for them at the table and invite them to sit and eat with us once more. The dumb part means that there is no talking during the meal. Talking sometimes frightens away ghosts, as you know from your ghost hunting. So we sit there without talking, or dumb."

She noticed Amber's continued frown and rushed on. "Dumb, a long time ago, didn't mean stupid. It meant not able to talk. Since we are not able to talk during this meal, we call it a Dumb Supper."

Amber's frown had disappeared so Rory thought she might have gotten through.

"That's what I'm having on Halloween, and you're all welcome to come and join me." She looked pointedly at Travis. "All of you."

"I don't know." Michael shook his head. "I usually take my brother and sister trick-or-treating. I'd like to come, but I can't miss that."

Rory smiled. "We can start the supper later if it's all right with your parents. You can do your usual Halloween stuff, and we'll meet around 8:30."

"Cool." Michael's face split into a grin. "That would be awesome."

"I can pick you guys up at the school again." Travis glanced over at her. "Meet me about 8:15, and you can tell your folks I'll have you home by ten."

"Awesome!" They all high-fived each other and ran off down the pier, throwing a "thanks, Ms. DuMont" back over their shoulders as they bumped their way through the crowd.

"Living dangerously these days, are you, Mr. Reed?" Rory looked up at him as he took her hand once again.

"Not at all. Just doing my part for the advancement of science."

"Two ghost hunts in one month. I don't know. If you keep this up, Jane Harvitz is going to be offering to sign you up as Lobster Cove's newest member of the Ghost Hunting Society."

Travis shuddered. "Don't even joke about something like that. I spent far too many nights as a kid listening to my parents and their friends arguing the finer points of astral travel and angelic spirit guides. Believe me, it sounded far more complicated than astrophysics."

"So you opted for the easy way out, is that it?"

"Yes, ma'am."

"Yet here you are with me."

"Yes, ma'am."

"Doesn't that make you wonder?"

"I always wonder about things."

"But I mean, shouldn't it make you wonder if being with me is the right thing for you?"

He stopped, tugging her hand until she turned to face him. "Rory, wondering is a good thing, a useful thing. But if all you do is wonder, it doesn't give you any answers."

She gave him a quizzical look and he laughed.

"You can spend your whole life wondering about stuff, about how something might fit or work out or come to be and that's good, that's a start. But it's only creating your hypothesis. If you never experiment, you will never know if what you wonder is true. You have to try it on, check it out, walk around in it a while to see how it fits."

"And that's what we're doing now?"

"Didn't you come all the way out here to try on Lobster Cove? It wasn't just your aunt's cottage that brought you here. If you didn't like the rest of it, you wouldn't stay. The cottage was the initial step, but you've taken it further. You're getting out, getting to know people, trying this town on to see how it fits."

"Okay, I can follow that. So you're spending time with me to try me on and see if I fit."

He gave her a wicked smile, and she turned red as she realized how her words sounded. Oh great, she thought, now I not only look crazy, I look needy.

"Let me rephrase that."

"No, that's okay. I think I got the gist of it. Look, Rory, let's try this on. We have some differences. One of the things my parents talked about endlessly that I didn't step away from was the beauty of diversity. Being different isn't the same as being incompatible. So let's take this one step at a time and see how it goes." He grinned at her. "You might just find we fit better than you think."

Chapter Six

It was late when they got back to the cottage. Rory's feet hurt, her stomach felt like it would explode and she was happier than she'd been in a very long time. Spending the day with Travis had been more fun than she expected and more eye-opening. It had been like examining him in his natural habitat. The conclusion was an easy one. People liked him. It was interesting to stand back and observe as he interacted with the parents of his students and with the students themselves. His easy manner was the same with the adults as it was with his kids. Watching him, Rory realized that he just liked people, and they liked him. He joked with them, complimented their kids, and gave them something to feel good about. She thought that probably didn't happen often to parents of middle school kids. Being rotten was often what they did best.

As he pushed open her door, Rory felt a strange current of energy hit her. All of her instincts told her it was ghostly energy, but she saw nothing. There was an odd tinge to the energy, not malevolent, or at least not entirely. But it carried a great deal of chaotic energy, sad and lonely and filled with a violent hue that streaked it with a taste of melancholy. Rory braced a hand on the doorframe as she stumbled through the door. Travis glanced down at her.

"Sleepy?"

"No." Rory shook her head, shoving the ghostly energy away for the moment. The day had been too perfect, too much fun to delve into that kind of melancholy now. "More worn out than sleepy. And content."

"Ah, so that's what that look is. I was afraid I might have bored you with all the talk about the oceanic studies."

"No, I enjoyed listening to you. The work you're doing is fascinating."

"I wish more of my students thought so."

"You're planting a seed. It'll just take time for it to grow."

"Now you sound like those teacher magazines."

Feeling very bold, she stood up on tiptoes and kissed him on the cheek. "Thank you for a wonderful day." She stepped back and smiled at the surprise on his face.

He pulled her back to him and kissed her back but it wasn't a simple, friendly one. It was a kiss that promised more, and it made her head spin. When he let her go it was all she could do to not go "wow."

"You're very welcome, Ms. DuMont. Believe me, it was my pleasure."

Well, that certainly put a cap on the weary feeling, she thought. Rory felt the heat on her face and decided she'd better put her packages down before they ended up on the floor. She dropped them on the overstuffed sofa then plopped down herself. As she leaned her head back against the soft cushion she groaned.

"Okay, now that I've sat down I'm feeling the burn. We did a lot of walking today. My muscles are now reminding me of the dangers of spending too much time hunched over my computer and not enough time stretching them out."

Travis dropped down onto the floor beside the sofa. "Come here."

He spread out his long legs, and Rory felt her mouth go dry. The last traces of fatigue vanished to be replaced by need, hot and heavy. He patted his knees. Rory arched a brow at him.

"Excuse me?"

Travis pointed to the spot on the floor in front of him. "Have a seat. You're about to receive the benefit of my mother's lifelong training in healing massage. I'm going to show your muscles they've got nothing to worry about so long as you have me around."

What about the rest of me? Rory wondered. His words had some other parts of her body clamoring for attention as well. Just the sight of him sitting there, like an offering of male sexuality laid out specifically for her, stirred up a hornet's nest of desire in every part of her body.

Ignoring the protests of her little inner voice, which was getting on her nerves more and more these days, Rory sank down between Travis' knees and leaned her head back against his chest. Surrounded by him, inhaling his scent, made her dizzy with the desire for more. He leaned over and kissed her.

"Just put yourself in my hands, Rory. Put your worries aside for now and let me make things better."

"Uh-huh." She almost whimpered as he started kneading her shoulders. "Who knew someone so dedicated to logic and reason could have such magical fingers."

"Nothing to do with magic. Everything to do with

biology."

"Less talk, more action, Teacher Man."

He chuckled. "Your call, Ms. DuMont. I aim to please."

"Then aim right here, please." Rory leaned forward and rubbed a hand along the back of her neck.

"Ah, in time." Travis pushed her head back down as his fingers slid up to tangle in her hair. "Tonight you get the full treatment."

His strong fingers flexed in her hair, warm and steady, filling her with a heat that spread through her tired body. Rory bit her lip as he rubbed her temples, willing herself to let go of the worry, let go of the fear and let things be. She listened to his breath, a steady sure sound that both calmed and stirred her. Travis was here right now, she told her inner voice. He was beside her, touching her, heating her with passion. Tonight, she thought, that was enough. Tomorrow could be worried about later.

She melted back against him as his hands made slow, soothing circles around her neck and shoulders. At first he was gentle, but as she relaxed against his chest, his hands became firmer, stroking up and around her shoulders before moving lower. Rory let out a soft sigh as his fingers dipped beneath the top of her blouse, scraping her sensitized skin with the rough pads of his fingertips.

"Umm..." Rory felt herself slip into the rhythmic movements of his hands, hypnotized by the feel of his palms kneading her muscles. "This is something your mother taught you?"

"I've added a few techniques of my own."

"I'll say."

Time slid away as she gave herself over to the feel of him stroking her. She let go of any thought but pleasure as she sat there, her mind doing a slow blur into a hazy world of sensual pleasure. The more his touch moved along her skin, the more she stretched out to give him other places to touch. He leaned over, and she shivered at the sensation of his hot breath on her skin. Keeping his hands moving, his fingers touching her sensitive spots, he pressed his lips to her neck, letting his tongue linger as he tasted her with slow, soft kisses.

He took her by the shoulders, urging her to turn and face him. Rory scooted around. Travis lifted her legs, placing one on each of his thighs. It was a surprisingly intimate position, Rory thought, one that put her in a good position to see the bulge in his jeans. Need and want and tenderness stirred up in her, and she found she wanted to take him inside her, to fill herself with him and give him all of her. Rory wasn't a virgin, but she always struggled with turning off her brain and letting the passion overwhelm her. Her previous relationships had had more going for them out of the bedroom than in. Worrying about the outcome generally had her measuring each move before she made it. This was the first time in her memory that placing herself in such an intimate situation didn't fill her with nervousness but instead flooded her with sheer unadulterated lust. Her mind actually let go of control and allowed her to be swept up in the passion of the moment. And let her participate in it. She wanted to rip his clothes off, to lean forward and take a bite out of him, and to love him with a tenderness she hadn't realized she possessed.

She couldn't take her eyes off his face, watching every expression that flitted across it as his fingers opened the buttons on her blouse one by one. The look of wonder in his eyes as the silk slid off her shoulders and fell to the floor, exposing her to his gaze, made the hunger inside her grow to a burning that fought to get out, to take control, to take what it wanted. To take him and make him her own.

Slowly Travis laid her back onto the floor, murmuring to her how beautiful she was as he did. His gaze roamed up and down the length of her, the desire filling those wild blue eyes exciting her on every level. For a moment she thought she could get lost in them, knew she would willingly jump into the passion they offered and go wherever the night took her. He was a man of such curiosity, and tonight she planned to let him do all the exploring he wanted. Tonight she understood the sensual side of that trait.

Travis leaned over her, and she smelled the ocean on him as he smoothed the rug out around her.

She wanted him close to her, weighting her down with his long lean body. Her fingers slipped under his t-shirt and stroked the hard muscles of his chest. His scent combined with the feel of his hot skin beneath her palms sent her senses into overload. She wanted to say something, but she wasn't certain her voice could form words anymore. All of her body had been reduced to its primal essence, to need straining to be filled, to be satisfied. Something about being on Aunt Lorena's rug with her body bared to the waist and her very own Viking warrior making her writhe beneath him had stolen the very breath out of her.

His fingers traced an expert line of desire down her

belly to reach for the snap of her jeans.

"You've done this before," she whispered.

He grinned, his fingers skimming below the band to slide along her hip. "All practice for now."

He covered her mouth with his own as his curious fingers splayed across her skin, and she bit back a moan. Rory let her head fall back as his hands slid her jeans and panties down to her knees. Before she could gasp he was cupping her, smoothing his rough palm over her mound in a motion that made her gasp. A look of pure male arrogance crossed his face at the sound. Then he thrust a finger inside her, and her mind left the room completely. The only thing left to do was to ride the current of the orgasm. When the waves of pleasure subsided, she looked up at a one very pleased man.

"Come here," she said, in perfect imitation of his invitation.

With a growl of frustrated need, she tugged at his shirt, and he obliged her by pulling it over his head. She wanted to lick him, bite him, have him cover her with all that hot muscle and take her on the wild ride those blue eyes promised. Sex wasn't foreign to her, but the feeling of being completely uninhibited with a naked man was. As the welcome sensation of pure pleasure rolled over her again, making her hot and needy beneath him, she hardly noticed him ridding her of the rest of her clothes. Her only thought was to get him out of the rest of his. Then her focus became a blur as he stroked her, tasted her, and growled with pure pleasure at the moans she couldn't hold back. Each new touch made her cry out for more even as he gave her so much sensual pleasure she thought she might explode from it. For a moment he held himself over her, as if commanding her complete attention. She might have told him he had it, but what came out of her mouth sounded more like a growl. Then he thrust inside her, fast and hard, in and out in the ancient rhythm of sex, building the flow of pure energy between them until she knew they would explode, couldn't help but explode from the power surging within their joined bodies. When the wave hit them, they rode it until it left them both spent and satisfied.

Rory was the first to get her breath back under control though it took far longer than it ever had before. Travis had shifted his weight off of her, but he lay with his eyes still closed, breathing heavily. It made Rory smile and made her feel a bit proud. I did that to him, she thought, with a mental pat on the back. When he finally rolled over beside her, curling her under his shoulder, she couldn't stop the smirk.

"Massage, huh?" She snorted as he grinned at her. "Mr. Reed, I'm thinking that kind of massage is illegal in most places."

"I'm working out the kinks in some of the adaptations I've made. You can think of yourself as my guinea pig."

"Now there's an image to spoil the moment."

"Sorry. My brain hasn't caught up with my mouth yet. Does research subject work better?"

"Slightly. That was the most thorough clinical examination I've ever had."

"I believe in having all the bases covered."

"Believe me, all my bases felt covered." And then some, she thought.

Rory cleared her throat. "You know though, the experiment will fail if you kill off your research subject."

"Death by sex. Not a bad way to go."

She wanted to laugh but didn't think she had the energy. As she sat up to pick up her blouse, she glanced around.

"I can't say much about your choice of lab facilities, although Aunt Lorena would love the way we put her rug to use."

"I do most of my best work in the field."

Travis sat up and took the blouse from her hands. She gave him a quizzical look and he grinned.

"I have another theory I want to check out."

"Theory?" Rory frowned. "Exactly what theory is that?"

"I've heard tell that witches use the elements in their magic. You know, things like earth, air, fire, water."

"And?"

"I thought I'd let you try some magic, so I could see how that sort of thing works. All in the interest of furthering scientific knowledge, of course."

"Of course. And what kind of magic am I supposed to do?"

"Well, since the earth and the air outside are a bit on the cold side, it being fall and all, and we've just successfully experimented with fire—"

"I'll say."

"I thought it was time to give water a try."

"Are you planning on throwing me in the ocean to see if I float?"

He reached for the blanket on the sofa and wrapped it around her. "We'll save that for another time. I thought we'd hit the shower and try a little magic in there."

"I'm really good with water magic."

"I thought you might be."

"Come on," she said, tugging him up. "And I'll show you just how good. You'll be a believer in magic before the night is through."

"I don't know. It might take a lot of persuading."

"It's Saturday. We've got all night."

"Yes, ma'am, we do."

Chapter Seven

Rory looked around the room, checking to see that everything was in order before her guests arrived. The old oak dining room table was set with Aunt Lorena's Limerick pattern china, eight place settings in all. Ireland seemed like the right addition to the night of All Hallows Eve. Maybe they'd see a leprechaun or one of the fey along with their ghostly guests, Rory thought with a grin. Dinner was warming in the oven, and the kitchen smelled nice and cozy. The sound of the October wind outside and the ocean waves crashing against the rocks below only added to the background ambiance.

She had opted for an altar to the dead for the table's centerpiece, knowing the kids would get a kick out of the melting skull candle with skeleton hands wrapped around it. Aunt Lorena's black silk tablecloth formed the perfect background for the deliciously creepy decorations. Down the length of the table, Rory had placed a strand of tiny orange pumpkin lights for added effect. Beneath each place setting lay a placemat of orange and black with dancing ghosts scattered across it, and in front of each plate sat a silver goblet shaped like a witch's cauldron. She had found a set of them on a trip to Salem with her aunt two years ago. They were a nice addition to her collection of Halloween kitsch. In the center of the altar was Rory's favorite photo of Aunt Lorena, taken the summer Rory had come to stay with her as a teenager. She found herself holding back a few tears as she gazed down at it.

"Thank you," she whispered to the photo. "For all of this."

As she heard the truck drive up, Rory lit the white candles around the edges of the table that had been the finishing touch on her altar. With a bit of pride she surveyed her setting.

"Well," she murmured, glancing around the room. "If no ghosts show up, then they're missing a great party."

She took a deep breath and sent up a whispered prayer that tonight would go well.

"Hello! We're here, ready or not."

Travis let out the greeting as they all tumbled through her door. The kids shrieked at the table setting, moving from place to place to check out the decorations. Rory hovered over them, fearful they would knock over the candles. Travis pulled her to him and gave her a kiss. Pulling back from her mouth he licked his lips.

"Mmm, you taste like chocolate. Sinfully sweet chocolate."

Rory laughed, wiping at the corner of her mouth to make sure there was no more evidence of her taste testing.

"You caught me. There's one of Bea's beautiful cakes in the fridge, waiting to become our dessert. Triple chocolate caramel."

"Wow." Travis let out an appreciative whistle. "Ghosts would be crazy not to show up. This is really a celebration then."

"Of course. I had to taste test a little bit of it, you know, to make sure it wasn't too sweet for the kids."

"And I'm sure their parents and their dentists appreciate your sacrifice."

"It was the adult thing to do, and since I was the only adult here, the sacrifice was mine to make."

"Yes indeed." Travis nodded solemnly. "Got to protect the poor kids from bad chocolate."

"My mother made sure my hostess skills were top of the line. Have to make her proud of me." With a grin, Rory turned back to the table. "Pictures?"

She held out her hand to the kids. After her initial invitation she had sent each kid a message through Travis asking all of them to bring a photo of a loved one who had passed on to be their "guest" at the supper.

"I brought my grandma." Amber produced a worn photo of a young girl with eyes the color of her granddaughter's and a face that was a near perfect twin to Amber's.

"That's your grandma?"

Michael grabbed at the picture with total confusion. Amber rolled her eyes.

"It's from when she was my age, dufus." She snatched the picture out of Michael's hands.

Rory showed Amber and Justin where to place their photos on the table. From his coat pocket Michael produced a small photo of a huge dog.

"I brought a photo of Regis."

"Your dog?" Amber frowned at him. "You were supposed to bring a picture of a person you loved who's died."

"Regis died last summer. And I loved him."

"A ghost of a dog isn't going to come to dinner."

Justin shook his head.

"Regis always sat by the table when we ate."

Michael glared at them stubbornly, clutching the photo tight in his hand. Rory glanced at Travis, who smothered his smile as he reached for Michael's photo.

"From what you've told me about Regis, Michael, he was a pretty smart dog. Seems to me if he gets a whiff of the dinner I'm smelling right now he'll show up for it."

"And he would be an honored guest," Rory added as Travis handed her the photo along with one of his own.

"My grandpa," he said. "My best fishing buddy."

Rory smiled at him as she placed it with the others on the altar.

When they were all seated around the table, Rory brought the turkey and the side dishes out to the accompaniment of oohhs and aahhs from everyone else. She had stuck to simple again since it worked so well the last time. As they all filled their plates, Rory took out a small bell and set it in front of her. She cleared her throat, and they all quieted down and looked at her.

"Remember when I told you that during this kind of supper you couldn't talk?"

They all nodded, serious as they had been the other night with all their ghost hunting equipment set up.

"When I ring the bell, it means the time for silence is started. That part of the dinner will last for thirty minutes while we wait to see if any of our guests show up. When the time is up, I'll ring the bell again and then you can talk."

Justin glanced around the room.

"Is it okay to eat after you ring the bell, or do we

have to sit here and wait for them to show up before we can eat?"

He looked concerned at what her answer might be, and Rory remembered how fast the other dinner she'd served them had disappeared. She shook her head.

"You don't have to wait." She wanted to laugh at the look of relief on all three faces.

"Go ahead and dig in as soon as I ring the bell. It's like eating dinner at home, just without the conversation. If you want something just reach for it. You don't have to ask. Just be careful of the candles."

They all nodded again, and Rory rang the bell. Across the table she could see the twinkle in Travis' eyes. He had wanted to bet with her earlier, certain none of the kids could keep quiet for that long. She hadn't been willing to take him up on the offer because she thought he was probably right.

The kids surprised them both though. There were a few missteps, especially when they reached for something across the table. Justin got out "ex" before he caught himself and Michael did whisper a quick "sorry" when he dropped the platter he'd been moving. Other than that they kept silent, their eyes darting around the room looking for ghost flashes as they called them. They had wanted to set up their equipment around the table, and Rory had to explain to them that this wasn't like one of their ghost hunting nights. It was a ritual of sorts, she'd told them, and it would be rude and disrespectful to treat it as anything less than a special meal to honor their ancestors. Hiding their reluctance, they agreed and left all their equipment at home. As she watched them now, Rory could tell they were mentally envisioning all the "data" they would have gotten with it set up.

Rory had told them she'd ring the bell in thirty minutes. It had been almost twenty when she heard the clatter of the bowl Amber had dropped. As she started to reach over and help her pick it up, Rory felt the otherworldly energy behind her. It felt benign at first, and she smiled at the thought that the kids might get something to talk about out of the evening after all. Then she noticed the look on Amber's face change just as the temperature in the room dropped noticeably. Shock didn't nearly cover the open-mouthed surprise on the girl's face. Michael dropped his spoon to the floor, and Justin stared past her with wide open eyes even as Rory picked up on the chaotic energy bursts beginning to fill the room. It was Travis', "What the hell?" that had Rory turning to look behind her.

The ghost girl was a young teenager, probably only a year or two older than the kids staring at her from the table. Her blonde hair hung down straight to her waist, and she was dressed in bell-bottom jeans and a black t-shirt. Bare feet peeked out from beneath the ragged hem of the jeans. And blood stained the leg of one side.

Her image was strong for a ghost, her features clear and sharp even by the candlelight. This was no weak wispy outline, but a force of energy that projected itself in a steady manner. There was no mistaking the pain on her face either. Rory tried to absorb the waves of it coming off the girl's ghost so the kids didn't get hit by it, but there was so much, she thought. So much anger and so much hurt.

Rory rose from the table even as Travis gathered the kids behind him. The look on his face was priceless. Shock warred with curiosity as both emotions moved across his features, and for a moment she feared he might try and touch the ghostly figure. Before he could do it, Rory stepped in front of him and turned to face the girl's image.

"It's okay." She spread her hands out in front of her in a gesture of calm as she kept her voice soft and even. "We're here to help."

The ghost girl mouthed the word back to her and Rory thought she added the word "me" to it.

"Help me. She said help me!"

Behind her Amber's voice rose excitedly, making the ghost shimmer and the waves of chaos coming off her rose until Rory thought she might fold under the rising strength of them.

"Shh."

Rory waved a hand behind her, never taking her gaze off the ethereal girl standing by her fireplace. The noise of scooting chairs and thumping feet told her the warning wasn't getting through. She turned back to see Travis stretching out an arm in front of the boys to keep them back. Amber had already moved up behind Rory. She leaned in against Rory's side and whispered.

"Is she hurt?"

Rory shook her head, but the ghost girl mouthed that word as well. *Hurt. Help me.*

Pain shot out from the ghost, deep, physical, and Rory sank down beneath the feel of it, pulling Amber down with her.

"She's hurt. We've got to help her."

Rory clasped a hand over Amber's mouth, earning her a glare. She turned back to the ghost to find the image wavering, the strength of the energy around it rising and roiling in a chaotic whirlwind. A moaning sound came out of the ghost's mouth, low at first but growing louder with each minute that passed. Rory glanced behind her and saw that the shock on the kids' faces had turned to fear. The moaning echoed off the walls of the tiny cottage to blend with the sound of the waves below, filling the space with an eerie energy.

Travis moved up behind her, and Amber and placed a hand on Rory's shoulder. She reached up and grasped his hand, letting him pull her back up. The sadness coming off the ghost broke over her, and Rory buried her face in Travis' shoulder. He wrapped one arm around her and the other around Amber, who had tears streaking down her face.

"We've got to do something!"

The panic in Amber's voice told Rory she needed to take control of the situation. Seeing a ghost was one thing, but having the kids go home and tell their parents they had been terrorized by one was another matter entirely. She took a slow step toward the ghost girl, her hands out in front of her.

"What can we do for you?"

Rory made her voice soft and non-threatening. The moaning stopped as the ghost girl stared at her.

Help me!

With that last cry, the image of their ghostly visitor vanished as quickly as it had come. The temperature in the room rose, and the only sounds they could hear was the roar of the ocean and their own breathing. Rory knew the ghost was gone. She turned back to the others. The boys still wore the look of stunned disbelief and tears rolled down Amber's face. It was the look of absolute and total shock on Travis' face that made her start to laugh.

"Welcome to my world, guys." Rory wiped the tears away from her own eyes as she got her laughter under control.

The kids looked at her with awe but Travis' face held consternation.

"This is what you see?" He croaked out the question then shook his head. "All the time?"

"Well," Rory smiled. "Not all the time. I saw my first spirit when I was five, although I didn't know at the time it was a spirit. I thought it was some kid from the neighborhood who had wandered in to play with me."

"You played with ghosts?" Michael's voice held deep respect.

"When I realized what they were I was a bit more careful," Rory confessed. "I found out not everyone saw them when I tried to introduce my new friend to my mother after she called me for lunch. My parents told me they were my imaginary playmates, and they strictly forbid me from talking about them."

"But that didn't keep you from seeing them, did it?" Travis' voice was quiet and thoughtful.

"No." Rory shook her head. "I still saw them, but I became very careful not to say anything to anyone else. At least, until Aunt Lorena came to visit."

"She saw them, too?" Justin stared at her.

"Yes. I was so grateful to have someone who understood what was going on. I looked forward to her visits each time because it was the only chance I got to talk about what was happening to me."

Rory looked at Travis when she said it, searching his face for any sign of rejection. His gaze never left her as he spoke.

"I can understand why she meant so much to you. It's always nice to be understood."

He moved to Rory, taking her into his arms. Understanding and acceptance were clear on his face. Rory nodded as she buried her face in his chest.

"Yes. Yes, it is."

"You guys!"

Amber's voice held annoyance and a trace of the sadness Rory had felt coming from the ghost. She turned to the girl, who stood staring at all of them with her hands on her hips.

"What is it, Amber?" Travis stepped back from Rory to look at his student. "Are you okay? It's over now, we can sit down. Don't worry about it. We can go home now if you want."

"No!" Amber stomped her foot with impatience. "It isn't over. You guys are just standing around talking like it is, and she's out there!"

For a moment Travis looked confused. "Who's out there?'

"She is! And she needs our help!"

Amber glared at all of them in turn. Rory reached for her hand, pulling her closer to them and away from the fireplace. There might be residual energy from their visitor hanging around there, and she thought it best to get Amber away from any of it. Clearly the ghost girl had had a big impact on the girl already. Amber shook off Rory's hand and continued glaring at them.

"She came here tonight to get our help. We can't just stand around here. We've got to do something!"

"Amber, she's a ghost." Rory said the words gently, hoping the girl would calm down and get her meaning. "You do understand what that means, don't you?"

"What it means is she needs us to help her. Somebody's hurting her, and we have to stop them."

"Amber." Travis pulled out a chair and motioned to her. "Come and sit down."

There was no mistaking the authority in his voice, and reluctantly Amber dropped into the chair. Travis pulled out chairs for Rory and himself then sat and faced the emotional young girl.

"I think what Rory is trying to tell you is that the…figure you saw was a ghost." He glanced over at Rory. "Although I'm reserving judgment on that, the point I believe she's trying to make is that the person that figure represents is already dead."

Amber looked at him. "So?"

"So, that means that whoever or whatever hurt her has already done so. She isn't around for us to help anymore."

Amber shook her head, tears starting down her cheeks again. "We have to help her." She turned a pleading look to Rory.

"Well," Rory sighed. "There is a way to help a spirit trapped here on earth by what happened to them."

Travis turned to frown at her. Justin and Michael, who had been quiet and still looked confused, turned to stare at her as well. Rory shrugged.

"It's something Aunt Lorena taught me to do. A way to give peace to those troubled spirits who couldn't move on." And this one certainly seems troubled, she thought, remembering the pain that had filled the room when the ghost started moaning.

"Like an exorcism?" Michael's look held both excitement and a bit of fear.

Justin smacked him on the shoulder. "That's demons, not ghosts. You don't have an exorcism for a ghost."

"No," Rory smiled. "Not an exorcism. Justin's right. Exorcisms aren't for ghosts."

"But isn't the only way to give her peace is to help her?" Amber's tear-stained face held a hopeful look.

"If by help her, you mean give her what she needs to move on, then yes. But Amber," Rory made her voice gentle. "Travis, um, Mr. Reed is right. Nothing we do can change what happened to whoever this girl was. It's too late for that. It's already happened."

"So we can't help her."

Rory wanted to tear up herself at the despair in Amber's voice. "We can do something to give her ghost some peace. That's helping."

"So what do we do?" Travis looked from her to Amber. "How do we help?"

"Well, the first thing we do, and the biggest problem we might face, is we need to know who this ghost is, or rather who she was."

"How do we find that out?"

Rory turned to Michael and smiled at him. It was nice to not have any of them running screaming out her door. She had expected the kids to take any paranormal activity they might see tonight as something cool and exciting. Not that she had expected anything near the magnitude of a completely visible ghost stand in front of them and plead for help. The person she hadn't expected acceptance from was Travis, yet he sat here with the rest of them, trying to figure out what they could do to help a ghost he didn't believe existed. Maybe the rejection would come later but for now she felt her attraction to him growing by leaps and bounds. If that attraction got shot down later she would worry about it then.

"Well, I'm not sure." She turned to Travis.

"I think this might be a job for some researchers." Travis said. "Probably the best place to start for that would be the library."

"The library can tell us who the ghost was?" Michael sounded confused as usual.

Travis laughed. "What the library has is old newspapers. From the looks of the blood on her clothes, this ghost girl must have been in an accident. So maybe there's a report of it in the newspapers."

Rory knew Travis was downplaying the scariest aspect of what they had seen. It wasn't a sure thing that the girl had been in an accident. She could very well have been murdered. But there was no sense scaring the kids more than they already had been with that kind of a scenario.

"Wouldn't we have read about an accident in the paper, though?" Justin asked.

Amber rolled her eyes at him. "It didn't happen yesterday. Didn't you see the way she looked?"

"Amber's right," Rory said. "This girl likely died a long time ago. From the way she was dressed I'd say maybe the 1960s or '70s." She turned to Travis. "Since you're the hippie expert I'll defer to you on that."

He nodded. "I think those years would be a good place to start based on her clothing. Although I guess some of that style could have stayed around for a while longer." He glanced over at the kids. "Or made a comeback later. But we can give it a try. How about it, guys? You up for some library time?"

The boys nodded and looked to Amber. She gave Rory a solemn look.

"And we can help her if we know who she was?"

"I think so." Rory reached over and squeezed Amber's hand. "I believe we can help her move on to a better place. Maybe even help her solve whatever kept her from moving on when she died."

"Okay." Amber nodded. "We go to the library then."

Chapter Eight

From the looks of him when he picked her up the next morning, Rory thought Travis must have had as sleepless a night as she did. She could just imagine the thoughts going through his logical mind. That wasn't a conversation she wanted to have at the moment, so she focused her own thoughts on how they might find the information that would identify their ghostly visitor.

The Lobster Cove Public Library was a pleasant surprise. Rory had expected a small cramped space without much in the way of research materials but instead found it to be a well thought out and well laid out building. Rachel Riley, the librarian on duty at the research desk when they arrived, was pleasant and helpful. Rory placed her in her late twenties or early thirties, which disappointed her. She'd secretly hoped the librarian would be a woman old enough to remember a young girl from the '70s dying in an accident. That would have made their search easier and quicker. Rory feared the longer it took them to find out who the ghost girl was the more the kids' active imaginations would build up a more dramatic scenario for her. Amber in particular was traumatized enough already.

Rachel told them she'd lived in Lobster Cove all her life, and when Rory said her name there was instant recognition. Nice to know the gossip about her hadn't died down yet, she thought. But it turned out that Rachel had known Rory's aunt.

"Ms. Lorena was in here all the time when she was in town." Rachel smiled. "She would give us lists of books she thought we should add to the collection."

"She loved to read." Rory nodded. "She was never without a recommendation for my reading list, and she was generally pretty insistent on her choices. Her reasoning was reading those books would make me well-rounded."

"That was the nice thing about Ms. Lorena's lists." Rachel laughed. "They covered a wide variety of topics. Most of the time our head librarian, Patsy Duncan, hated to get recommendations from people because they're usually books that are too expensive or too obscure. But Ms. Lorena would purchase them and donate them to the library if they were very expensive. We added some neat literature to our collection from her purchases."

"She was a big supporter of public libraries. One time she told me they were like banks and as important to a community as any financial institutions. They held the currency of knowledge, and that was more valuable than money."

"That sounds like her." Rachel agreed "She believed in education, and she believed in Lobster Cove. She is very much missed. We were all so glad when someone came to live in her cottage though. It would've been a shame to lose that piece of Lobster Cove's history."

Thankfully Travis had a library card so they could gain access to the files of old newspapers. Rachel showed them to the microfiche room, and they settled down to view the papers from the 1970s, thinking to start there first. It was a bit of luck that Lobster Cove had only had one newspaper back then. Thank goodness for small towns, Rory thought. Although there had been others during the town's history they had come and gone before the 1950s. That cut down on the material they would need to go through, although if they found nothing in the Lobster Cove papers Rory wasn't sure they wanted to tackle the larger Maine newspapers. That could take quite a bit of time and effort. She had some other thoughts on how to move their hurting spirit on if they couldn't find out who she was.

They hadn't had a chance to talk about the ghost on Friday night. Travis had taken the kids home and talked with their parents a bit about what had happened. Rory wondered how much he had downplayed things in order not to frighten their parents but to her surprise he had told them everything. That should keep her being the talk of the town for a long time. According to Travis, they took it well. She hoped he was right. Since each of the kids' families had relatives who were part of the Ghost Hunting Society, she guessed that should have been expected. Maybe she should be more worried about adults showing up to ghost hunt at the cottage.

The kids were going to search out the newspapers in the school library on Monday. Travis decided they could do the work as part of the grade they had missed when they skipped out of their ocean studies to ghost hunt. Rory told him he'd finally agreed with her philosophy, that if you couldn't beat 'em then join 'em, but he only smiled and stuck to his story that it was a good teaching technique. They hadn't talked about what had happened at the Dumb Supper, a fact that worried Rory a bit. Travis hadn't said anything negative but she wondered if that was coming when they did talk. Seeing a ghost you don't believe in had to be a traumatic change of events for a logical, reasonable person.

After three hours of staring at the screen, Rory was ready to give up hope they would find anything. She stretched and yawned before leaning over to look at the screen in front of Travis. He had a look of fascination on his face and she thought he might have found something but the only thing she saw was a page full of advertisements.

"What are you staring at?"

"Look at this," he said, pointing at the screen.

"You found something?" Rory looked harder at the blurred images. "Did you get her name?"

"Whose name?"

Travis turned a confused look to her, and Rory rolled her eyes.

"The name of the girl we've been sitting here looking for for the last three hours."

"Oh. Yeah. No, I didn't find her but look at this. Look at the prices on this stuff."

"Is that what you're gaping at? Advertisements?"

"Wow, stuff was cheap then."

She shook her head. "I'm sure they didn't think it was cheap. What was the minimum wage then, two, three bucks an hour?"

"Yeah, I guess you're right. It just seems crazy how much things have gone up." He looked over at Rory. "Why don't we take a break? You look hungry."

"I think that's your stomach growling, not mine. But a break sounds good."

"We can check out the Saturday special at Maggie's Diner then maybe we should go over and talk to Daryl Johnson."

"And he is?"

"Daryl is chief of police. He's been at it since before I was born. Maybe he'd remember something about a girl and an accident."

"That would be nice. I'm beginning to believe we're looking for a needle in a haystack."

They thanked Rachel on the way out and told her they might be back in an hour or so. Maggie's Diner was one of the eating places Rory had on her list to check out, so lunch sounded like the best thing right now. Travis' stomach may have been the one growling but she was sure hers wasn't far behind. The diner was an easy walk across the town square from the library, and it gave them the chance to stretch out the kinks from sitting bent over the microfiche machines.

"You know," Rory said, deciding to plunge ahead with what she knew needed to be talked about. "We haven't discussed what happened last night."

"It seems what happened last night has been our focus all day today. What is there to discuss beyond what we're doing now?"

She stopped and made him turn to her and stop as well. "Did you just try to avoid my question?"

Travis sighed. "Not really avoid it. Just defer it."

"Well, you're not getting a deferment on this one, Mr. Reed."

"How about a postponement? At least until we've ordered lunch."

Rory nodded, but the worry inside her bloomed to epic proportions. Food didn't seem like such a good idea now since nerves were wrecking havoc with her stomach. *You know you were expecting this. It was only a matter of time.* She tried to ignore her inner voice but the nagging doubts tormented her anyway.

Maggie's Diner was as cute inside as it had looked from the outside. The pretty blue-checked curtains on the windows matched the blue vinyl booths, and the cream and chrome tables looked very retro. The place was bustling with Saturday traffic, always a good sign in a restaurant in Rory's opinion. Travis waved to the harried waitress, who motioned them to a booth by the window. The menus were in little holders on the tables, and Rory pulled one out. All of it sounded delicious but she thought, when in Maine, so she decided on the lobster burger. Travis decided on the same. When they'd given the waitress their orders, Rory looked him in the eye.

"We haven't talked about the fact that we all saw a ghost. That *you* saw a ghost. And we need to."

He nodded. "Yes, I guess we do." For a moment he just looked at her, that thoughtful expression back on his face. "I can't say what happened, what I saw last night, didn't throw me for a loop. It's a bit hard to maintain a detached composure when you're looking right at something you didn't think existed."

Well, he'd spelled it all out, Rory thought. She had expected to have to coax that conclusion out of him.

"But?"

He let her question linger between them for a long minute. "But I also have excellent eyesight. Just had it checked last month, as a matter of fact. I know what I saw, there's no getting around that."

Rory blew out a breath. "If it helps, Aunt Lorena

explained it to me as a collection of kinetic energy gathering together in one spot to form an outline visible to the human eye."

Travis snorted. "It was a ghost, Rory. I understand what you're saying, but what I have to wrap my mind around is the visual of a young girl standing in your living room begging us to help her."

"Yes. That's pretty much the sum of it."

"Something else I'm wrapping my mind around is the fact that this is something that happens to you a lot."

Here it comes, Rory thought, steeling herself to see the rejection in his eyes. "Not every day but yes, it happens a lot. It's been this way since I was a kid, so I guess I've gotten used to it. They aren't all as serious as this. As a matter of fact, most of the sightings I have are pretty benign. Most of the time ghosts just want to check us out, take a look at what we're doing. Aunt Lorena taught me that spirits who stay around in places familiar to them do so because they enjoy the feel of being somewhere that feels like home. Eventually most of them move on. The ones you hear stories about who have lingered for years generally have some issue with moving on."

"Like this girl."

Rory nodded. "Yes, I'd say she has some issue with moving on, something preventing her from passing fully out of this world. It can be anything from a desire to talk to someone they knew one last time to residual trauma from the manner of their death."

Their food arrived, and Rory found herself grateful for the interruption. She could remain clinical about things for only so long. The burgers tasted delicious, but after a couple of bites, she put hers down and looked over at Travis.

"I can give you clinical descriptions all night long. What I can't do is ignore the fact that…things may have changed between us because of last night. Believe me, I know from personal experience what seeing something like that can do. If you would rather not—"

"Rory."

She paused at the serious tone in his voice, keeping her gaze down on the table.

"Look at me, Rory."

With a sigh she looked up at him. He shook his head.

"I've spent all day staring at a tiny computer screen full of grainy, barely visible images just so I could try and find a photo of a ghost. Do you really think I would have wasted my Saturday morning that way if I were ready to run from you?"

From the look on his face, Rory could tell he meant what he said.

"I'm going to say no."

"Good." This time his voice was fierce. "That answer gives me hope that we can put this issue to rest once and for all. If there ever comes a time when I'm ready to throw in the towel, and I do not see that option as ever being viable, it won't be because I'm scared of who you are or of what you are. Both of those things are what attracted me to you. So stop worrying."

"Okay." She nodded.

"Now eat up. We've got a picture to find."

Chapter Nine

It turned out they didn't have to spend more hours in front of the microfiche machines. Instead of going back to the library right after lunch, Travis decided they should stop at the police chief's house first. The decision turned out to be a good one.

"Yeah, I think I might know who you're talking about."

They were in Chief Johnson's cramped home office. Rory and Travis had given him a detailed description of the ghost girl and told him they thought she had been in an accident. The part they omitted was the truth about why they wanted to find her. Rory insisted they leave out the ghost part, and Travis seemed more than willing to agree to that. Instead, they told Chief Johnson the research was part of a history of Lobster Cove that Rory wanted to write, and that she had found a description of the girl in her aunt's journals.

Johnson had an entire wall of file cabinets filled with files and clippings from cases going back to his early days as chief. He dug through one cabinet, mumbling to himself as he shuffled through the tightly filled drawer before pulling out a worn green folder.

"This should be it."

Rory held her breath as she and Travis leaned over the man's shoulder while he turned the fragile newspaper clippings in the folder. The last article in the pile had them both gasping.

It was definitely their ghost girl in the grainy photo. She was wearing the same clothes they'd seen her in last night, but she looked younger, happier than the face she'd shown them at the Dumb Supper.

"Laurel Gardner." Travis read the name off the article. "She was fifteen."

"I remember this one," Chief Johnson added. "She was a runaway, came down from Augusta."

Rory turned the page over to check the date. "August 10th, 1971. That explains the clothes."

"Original, not retro," Travis added. "Did they find her? Or her body?"

Chief Johnson shook his head. "No, that was what made it stick in my head. A couple of people saw her in town, but when the bulletin came through, she had either moved on or…"

"Or passed on." Rory felt her throat tighten at the words. *Had Laurel Gardner died right here in Lobster Cove?* The year wasn't long ago enough that the thought of a murderer in the little town didn't give her the shivers. *What if someone had killed her and never been caught?*

He nodded. "We searched the coastline, even dragged Grant's Lake but never found any sign of her. I felt sorry for her poor family.

"You met them?" Rory asked.

"They came here when the bulletin came out saying she'd been sighted in Lobster Cove. Father, mother and an older sibling—a sister, if I remember right. Stayed for nearly two weeks, walking all over the town. Young kid like that, you just knew they thought she was dead. The bulletin gave them hope, but…nothing came of it."

He made them a copy of the article on his little printer. Rory and Travis thanked him for the help and Rory promised to let him have a copy of the book when she got it written. She felt a bit guilty lying to the man but didn't know what else to say when he asked.

"Well, what now?" Travis asked her, as they got back into his car.

"We know who she was, and we know how she got to Lobster Cove."

"Is that enough to put her to rest?"

Rory bit her lip as she thought about a ritual that might soothe their ghost girl. Something still nagged at her though. Finally she shook her head.

"I don't think so. We don't know what happened to Laurel. If she was in as much pain as it looked like last night, just wishing her well isn't going to change that."

"So she'll stick around…because of the trauma, like you said." Travis stared down at the picture in her hand. "Doesn't seem like we've found out what we need to know yet."

"No, it doesn't." Rory sighed.

"Then what's the next step, Ms. Ghost Hunter?"

"We find out what happened to Laurel Gardner."

He raised a brow. "You do understand that was a lot of years ago. You did hear the part about how they looked all over town back then and didn't find a trace of her, right?"

"Uh-huh, I heard that. I guess it's possible that she moved on after being spotted in Lobster Cove. It's also possible that they missed her."

"And if she didn't stay in Lobster Cove? Or died

here? How do we go about finding her all these years later when we don't even know the answer to those questions?"

"It's not going to be easy."

"That's a bit of an understatement."

"I do have an idea that might help us get that answer." She glanced over at him. "It would mean doing something that might make you uncomfortable again."

"I'm getting used to that. Guessing it sort of comes with the territory. Historically, witches didn't tend to make people comfortable."

"This is going to stretch the territory a bit. And your comfort level."

"More than you've already stretched it?"

"Uh-huh. I think we need some help."

"That's your idea? That doesn't take me out of my comfort zone so much as out of my how-do-I-be-polite-when-I answer zone."

"Don't be a smart-ass. What I'm talking about is help from someone who has a better chance of getting the information from a very reliable source."

"And that would be?"

"Laurel herself."

Travis pulled into her driveway and shut off the car before turning to stare at her. "You're not talking about contacting a medium are you?"

Rory wanted to giggle at the horrified look on his face. Part of her thought she should tell him yes just to enjoy his reaction. But the kinder part of her won out. She shook her head.

"No, no medium. I'm not talking about holding a séance, just a ritual."

"A ritual? Do we get to dance naked by the ocean?"

"We can save that for later. That's more of a Beltane thing. Besides, it's a bit cold outside at night for the naked part."

"I can show you a way to warm up. Remember I said dance?" He wiggled his eyebrows.

She snorted. "You are far too into that concept. You've clearly never done the actual deed, especially not in winter. Believe me, there are drawbacks to being completely naked out in nature. Things like bugs, sand, cold, too much sun, too little sun."

"You don't sound like a very good witch to me."

"I didn't say there weren't benefits to it. I'm just recommending careful selection of the location. Besides, there is enough talk about me as it is. I'm not adding skyclad rituals by the ocean to that gossip."

"You really don't know how to live dangerously, do you? What good is gossip if it isn't juicy and *risqué*?"

"Exactly my point. I want everyone to get tired of talking about me so I can do what I want without worrying about excess attention."

"I can give you excess attention."

"We can discuss that if you stick around after what I'm planning."

"Which is a ritual. Are we going to summon a demon or something?"

"Witches don't believe in demons. And you don't sound like you're taking this very seriously."

"Then who are you planning on calling on to give you information on Laurel? And my head is still spinning from seeing a ghost. Give me time to recover.

I'll be serious later."

"Fair enough. But this might set your recovery back a bit. I can do the ritual myself if you'd prefer that."

"I'm a scientist, remember? No experimenting without me."

"Are you up for it tonight? It would be better for all of us, I think, if we got this matter settled right away."

"Absolutely. Up for what? I'd like a few more details of exactly what to prepare my recovering psyche for."

"A ritual to Hecate."

"Who?"

"Hecate. She is a primal Goddess, usually associated with crossroads."

"And lost girls?"

"Sometimes. It's more that she is good at crime scenes."

"Didn't know there were many crime scenes back in the old days. The really old days."

"There have always been crime scenes. Don't you remember Cain and Abel?"

"Different religion, so I didn't think they applied."

Rory opened the car door. "I need to gather a few things to prepare for the ritual. And it needs to be dark. Why don't you meet me back here around nine tonight?"

"Do I need to wear anything special?"

"Just some heavy duty armor around your psyche."

"Gotcha."

Rory shook her head as he drove off. "No, I've got you," she murmured. "And the real surprise of that is you just might stick around." That was definitely something for her to think about.

Chapter Ten

The moon was full and bright over the ocean as Rory set her circle. She'd selected a nice smooth area mostly free from rocks, at least large ones. It was a spot she'd been planning to make into a permanent circle since she'd moved into the cottage. Her Wiccan practice had taught her the value of having a space dedicated to ritual and spellwork. Aunt Lorena had not been Wiccan, so there was no spot already dedicated. Her aunt had dealt only in helping troubled spirits and generally that did not require a circle.

She'd bathed and done the cleansing that put her mind in the frame needed for sacred work. Dressed in the long black robe she used for night magic, she swept the circle space with her besom and got out the rest of her supplies. In the center of the circle, she built a spider's web with black yarn, positioning three black candles in a triangle at the center of the web. She placed the photo of Laurel Gardner in the center of the candles.

As she stood up she saw Travis making his way over the rocks. It didn't help the adrenalin rushing through her to watch him striding over them with the ocean waves crashing behind him. He was dressed in black as well and looked very much like a pirate come to pillage and ravish. Ravish would be very nice at this point, she thought. Her sensible side told her sex magic wouldn't be the best option in this instance, damn the luck.

"Wow." Travis whistled. "That looks pretty eerie."

He walked a few feet around the space before stopping to look at her. "I'm not messing anything up, am I? I mean, I didn't mess with the aura or the energy or the what not by walking around?"

"No, you're fine." Rory smiled at him, glad he'd decided to be here, grateful he hadn't run and totally bewildered by that fact at the same time. "The circle isn't cast yet, so you're fine to walk around."

"So what do we do next?"

"Well, everything is set up so we can get started whenever you're ready. It helps that the moon is so bright tonight. The candles aren't much light so the extra will be nice."

"Never fear, I come prepared." Travis pulled a flashlight out of the pocket of his coat. "Don't want to break a leg stumbling on these rocks in the dark."

"No, that would not be good. I'll cast the circle and once I do, you just need to stay inside it. You can help me build the circle by focusing your thoughts, imagining a circle in your mind. That adds to the energy. After it's cast, I'll call on Hecate to speak to us and ask her to find Laurel."

Travis took a deep breath. "Sounds pretty simple. Okay, let's do it."

Rory nodded and closed her eyes, pulling the energy up from the ground beneath her. When she felt it connect with her own energy, she began to walk the circle she'd laid out, seeing it grow in her mind. She could feel the energy rolling off Travis. It was a shame he wasn't Wiccan for his energy was strong and clear. As she completed the walk around, she added a quick prayer to her patron Goddess Brighid, thanking her for the protection of her circle this night.

She opened her eyes to find Travis staring at her. The look on his face told her he felt the energy and didn't know quite what to do with it. Hold on, she thought, things are going to get a bit bumpier before we're done. All she could do was smile at him and hope he hung in there. Rory moved to the center of the circle and lit the candles waiting in the web.

The moon hung over them, and she could feel the power building as the tiny flames caught and bloomed. Holding a hand palm down over the center of it, Rory walked around the web of yarn.

"Great Goddess Hecate, Mother of the Night and Guardian of the Crossroads, we come to you this night seeking one who is lost, one who is hurt, one who wanders in your domain seeking help and solace. We wish to heal her pain and guide her home and ask that you show us how to reach Laurel Gardner."

As soon as she said the young girl's name, Rory felt a strange stab of pain hit her heart. She opened her eyes, searching the dark around her. The energy was not exactly ghostly but it held the same pain that Laurel had brought with her the night she'd appeared to them. Something, or someone watched them from outside her circle, of that Rory was certain. She glanced over at Travis, whose gaze was searching the surrounding area as well. From the look on his face, Rory could tell he felt the strangeness around them, too. Whoever it was stayed well-hidden in the shadows. Turning her attention back to the web, Rory raised her hands to the sky and pulled the energy down from the silver moon.

"Laurel Gardner, we wish you peace. We offer you

our help for your journey. In this circle, this night the domain of the Great Mother Hecate, we ask you to reveal yourself to us."

Rory's words barely had time to echo in the circle and there she was. Laurel stood in front of the web, gazing at them, eyes filled with pain. It took Rory a moment to realize that the sobbing that rose up in the night wasn't coming from the ghost in front of them.

She lifted her gaze to the rocks around them and gasped. Travis turned to see where she was looking. Right outside their circle stood Margaret Vincent. Margaret's eyes were glued to the ghostly figure in front of the web. Rory could only watch and wonder as the ghost of Laurel Gardner turned to Margaret and smiled. Some of the pain left the ghostly eyes as the young girl stared at the older woman with what Rory knew in her gut was longing. Travis started to move, and she motioned to him to be still.

Heedless of both Rory and Travis, Margaret moved into the circle, reaching out a hand toward the young girl who still smiled at her. Tears streamed down Margaret's face, and her sobs broke Rory's heart. Whatever the connection between them, the pain rolling out of Margaret was deep and very, very real. Before Margaret could touch her, Laurel turned back to Rory and beckoned her with one ghostly hand. Not waiting for an answer, the ghostly image moved out of the circle and down the rocky shoreline. With a glance at Travis, Rory moved to follow. As she passed Margaret the woman turned wild eyes up to her.

"Come on," Rory whispered. "She's going to show us where she is."

Travis took Margaret's arm as they stumbled their

way down the rocks and sand. At first Rory thought Laurel was leading them into the ocean. She almost turned and told Travis and Margaret to go back, but the ghost girl started back up the rocky shore before Rory could say anything.

They had gone nearly fifty yards from the circle when Laurel led them to a tiny overhang, a rock shelter that had been eroded by the tide over many years. Laurel stopped and waited for them to come up to the shelter, her hand waving to urge them onward. Anticipation tingled in the air around them, and Rory knew they were close to the place that had kept Laurel bound to Lobster Cove all these years.

Travis let go of Margaret and knelt by the opening.

"Stay here for a minute, and I'll take a look."

Rory nodded, reaching over to hold Margaret's hand. To her surprise the woman let her take it without complaint. Her tears had slowed, but the heartache still rolled off her in waves. They could see the reflection of Travis' flashlight bouncing off the rock walls of the overhang. Margaret's hand was cold in hers. Rory cupped it in her fingers, rubbing her other hand along Margaret's back.

"It's okay. Everything's going to be okay now."

Margaret gave her a mute nod, the bleak look in her eyes cutting Rory straight to the heart. Rory had a sudden fear. *Was it possible Margaret was responsible for Laurel's death? Was it guilt that brought her here?* Rory thought back to the day she'd seen Margaret by the ocean. The pain had been there that day, too. What was behind that hurt, she wondered. Guilt? Regret? Or something far more sinister.

Travis reappeared at the opening, and his gaze

caught Rory's. With a small cry, Margaret started to move past him and he blocked her.

"We're going to need to call the sheriff."

"The sheriff? You found something then." Rory searched his face for her answer.

Travis nodded. "Yes. And I found this."

In his hand he held a yellowed piece of paper. It looked like the kind you tore from a spiral notebook but it had clearly been in the weather for a long time.

"I almost didn't see it after I...it was under a rock, like someone...like she put it there so it wouldn't blow away or wash away." He looked at Rory and she could see the sadness in his eyes. "Like it was important to her that someone find it one day."

"Or find her," Rory murmured.

"Yeah," he nodded. "I'm sure she hoped someone would find her one day."

"And did we find her?"

He nodded. "Yeah, she's in there. Or I'm guessing it's her."

Rory pointed to the paper in his hand. "The note doesn't tell you?"

"No." Travis looked confused as he glanced down at the paper. "The note doesn't say much, and it doesn't have a name. That's why it was so odd she made sure to keep it safe."

"Well, what does it say?"

Rory took the slip of paper from him and read the single line scrawled across it.

Guess you were right about how clumsy I am, Meg.

Before Rory had a chance to comment on the strange words, Margaret let out a long low cry then fainted dead away.

Chapter Eleven

Sheriff Lynn Lawton-Mackenzie stared at them with hard gray-green eyes that betrayed none of the incredulity that was clear in her voice. She was a slender, no-nonsense woman who looked like she was having a difficult time believing why she was standing out by the shore on a cold November night.

"You followed a ghost here."

She looked from Travis to Rory and back to Travis. He nodded.

"Yeah. We kinda held a...thing...to call up the ghost cause...we..."

He looked helplessly over at Rory.

"Sheriff, I know it's not your usual middle of the night call. But back on Samhain—"

"Halloween?"

"Yes." Rory stared at the sheriff in surprise. "Yes, Samhain is the Wiccan name for the night of Halloween. Back on Samhain we saw the ghost of a young girl, a girl we later found out was named Laurel Gardner. She went missing back in 1971, and she was last seen in Lobster Cove."

"And you found this out how?"

Rory noticed the sheriff's pencil was still poised over her notebook. She'd written down nothing they had told her so far.

"Daryl Johnson had a picture of her...of the ghost

we'd seen, in his files."

Rory breathed a sigh of relief when Travis took over the story. Surely the sheriff would listen to him more than her. He was the scientist, after all.

"Daryl had a picture of a ghost." The sheriff still seemed skeptical.

"It was an old newspaper clipping about how she'd run away that summer and been seen in Lobster Cove."

"So you came down here to check it out?"

"We saw her again tonight."

"You and Ms. DuMont."

"And Margaret, too. Margaret Vincent."

Sheriff Lawton-Mackenzie glanced over at Margaret, who sat on a large rock, staring out at the ocean. Though both Rory and Travis tried asking her a number of questions, she hadn't said a word since she came out of the faint. She'd moved over to a boulder near the front of the overhang, sat down, and stared out at the ocean.

"Okay." The sheriff closed her notebook and tucked the pencil into her dark hair. "Let's see what you found. We'll talk more about how you found it later."

And won't that be fun, thought Rory as she followed Travis and the sheriff into the rocky shelter.

Her bones lay against the back wall, as if she had fallen asleep as far from the opening as she could. The spot was just barely out of reach of the tide's movements. Her hiding spot was hardly big enough to have kept her sheltered at all. Rory wondered why she would have chosen such a spot, hidden but not really safe. *Or was it chosen for her by whoever left her here?* She thought of Margaret, sitting outside the shelter like a sentinel. In spite of all they'd done this evening, it seemed there were still a great many unanswered questions.

The sheriff's practiced eye quickly scanned the scene then she ordered them all out.

"I don't want anyone else coming in here until I get a forensics team out here."

****

Rory brought the steaming cup to the table and handed it to Margaret. She and Travis had talked Margaret into coming inside though it had taken the persuasive powers of both and the arrival of the forensics team to convince her. She had watched the team set up their equipment for a moment before letting out a low sob and turning to walk back up the slope.

"Here you go." Rory wrapped Margaret's hand around the warm cup. "This will warm you up in no time."

Since she'd come inside, Margaret had stopped crying. Now she just looked lost. Travis was sitting beside her, holding one of her hands in his. She looked from him to Rory and back.

"I guess I should explain."

Rory sat down on the other side of her. "Talk if you want to but you don't have to."

Margaret sighed. "I'll have to explain it to the sheriff anyway. I might as well explain it to both of you, too. It'll help me clear my thoughts for later."

She lifted the cup to her lips and took a sip. After placing it back on the table she looked over at Rory.

"First I want to thank you."

"Thank me?"

"For finding her. For finding Laurel."

"You're welcome."

"You did something I've been trying to do for a lot of years."

"She was your sister, wasn't she? You're Meg."

Margaret nodded, and Rory saw the tears gathering in her eyes again.

"I moved to Lobster Cove more than twenty-five years ago, but it wasn't the first time I'd been here."

"The first time was in 1971, when you and your parents came to look for Laurel."

"Yes. It had been nearly a month since she'd run away, and my parents had lost hope. When they heard she'd been spotted in Lobster Cove, they were so excited. We came down right away, but it was too late. She'd gone, or so we thought."

"But you came back."

"After Lobster Cove there were no more sightings of Laurel. It was like she'd dropped off the face of the earth. We never heard from her again. My parents were devastated. They never recovered from losing her."

"That must have made it hard for you.

Margaret gave Travis a weak smile. "Harder to live with the fact that I was the reason she left." She shook her head. "We had argued, we always did. I was eighteen, and she was fifteen. It doesn't sound like much difference, but in temperament we were worlds apart. But this time it was so much worse. She was…wild. My parents were older, had been in their forties when Laurel and I were born. By the time she reached her teens they had little control over her."

"And it was the 70s."

"And it was the 70s. The whole world had gone wild, I guess. Laurel had friends, lots of them, and she liked to party. That night she'd come creeping in from another party she had snuck out to. I knew Mom and Dad were at their wits end. When she came stumbling into the house that night she knocked over a vase, one that had belonged to Grandma Rosen. I knew Mom treasured it and seeing it lying there in pieces on the floor, I just snapped. I don't even remember what all I said to her." She gave a bitter laugh as she pointed to the faded note lying on the table. "I guess I called her clumsy. She was drunk or high or maybe both, I don't know. As usual she called me a few choice names and went to her room and slammed the door. I cleaned up the vase and tried not to think about the scene that would come in the morning. But by morning she was gone."

"And you never saw her again."

Travis' voice was gentle, but Margaret started to shake as the tears rolled freely down her cheeks.

"No. Yes. I did see her again, just not in the way I expected."

"You saw her ghost."

She nodded at Rory. "Yes. After we got back to Augusta, I tried the best I could to take care of Mom and Dad. But neither of them ever recovered. They died within two years of each other. I'd married by then, but my marriage fell apart after a couple of years." Margaret looked down at her hands. "Fell apart isn't really right. Tonight is a night for hard truths. My husband left me because of my drinking. I don't know how it started. Maybe it was taking care of my parents, maybe it was wondering what I could have done differently. A little drink here and there seemed to help make it all easier. I don't think I realized how my little drinks had become more and more often until James left."

"So you came to Lobster Cove?"

"I was driving through the summer after my divorce was final. Before I headed out of town, I stopped my car down by the lighthouse, to walk along the shore. I don't know if something drew me there or not, but I found myself thinking about Laurel. All the memories flooded over me, and when I looked up, she was standing there, dressed just like she was tonight. She didn't say anything, just stared at me. But I knew, I knew she was here, somewhere, still in Lobster Cove." She sighed. "I went back home, packed up my things, and moved down here."

"And you searched for her. That day I saw you, you were looking for her, weren't you?"

"Yes. It was like I wanted to stay away, but I couldn't. I'd look for her then I'd try and stay away from the ocean, away from where I knew she was. If I found her, I knew she'd be..."

"You knew she was dead." Rory took Margaret's hand and held on as the grief rode her.

"Wondering what happened to her just made it worse." Margaret sighed. "It would be good to know."

"I might be able to help you with that."

None of them had heard the sheriff come in until she spoke. Margaret stared up at her.

"The forensics team is finishing up. They'll take...the remains to the lab in Bar Harbor. We don't have the facilities here to confirm things like identity and cause of death."

"How long before they know something?" Travis asked.

"Well, first we have to make sure this is Laurel

Gardner. We'll need dental records to confirm."

Margaret nodded. "I can get you what you need."

"But the letter does seem to point to it being Laurel, right?" Rory fingered the yellowed paper. Everyone involved needed closure and her hope was the forensics would give it to them.

Sheriff Lawton-Mackenzie nodded. "It's a start. We have to have official confirmation though, and we need to know what happened to her."

"You said something about maybe being able to answer that." Travis gave the sheriff a quizzical look.

"The head of the team did say that although he couldn't give an official finding, it looked to him like whoever it was broke their leg."

"She broke her leg?"

"Yes. It could have happened out there on the shore and for whatever reason, the person didn't have a way to get to help."

"My aunt did a lot of traveling. She may have been gone. I've wondered why Laurel never connected with her, but I found no mention of her in any of my aunt's journals."

"Back in those days there weren't things like cell phones either. So injured, hurting, whoever it was likely found a place to hole up and wasn't able to get out again." Sheriff Lawton's gaze shifted to Margaret and Rory saw kindness in it. "Like I said, it's not official yet."

Margaret nodded to her. "Thank you, Lynn. If it turns out to…be Laurel, I'll take care of things from there."

"Okay. Like I said, the team is loading up now. They should be out of here in another half hour or so."

Rory looked at Margaret. "You're welcome to stay here, Margaret. The other bedroom is comfy."

She shook her head. "I think I'd like to go home. It's been a long night."

Travis rose from the table. "I can give you a ride home then. We can bring you back tomorrow for your car."

Margaret nodded, still lost in her grief as she followed the sheriff out the door. Travis pulled Rory to him and gave her a kiss.

"It's been a long night for all of us."

"Yes." Rory buried her face in his shirt, inhaling the scent of him. "Yes, it has."

Travis tilted her face up and smiled down at her. "I'll be back. I'm not leaving you alone tonight. So if you have a problem with that you'd better speak up now."

"No problem." As she gazed up at him a slow smile spread across her face. "You stayed. You've seen a ghost, did a ritual and you stayed."

He cupped her face in his hands before lowering his mouth to hers. Rory let herself sink into the kiss, let it soothe and stir her, enjoying the taste of him, the feel of him. His arms slid around her and a feeling of safety that she had never known before welled up in her. For a moment she let herself rest in it. When he finally stepped back from her, Rory found there were tears in her eyes. Travis wiped her cheeks and smiled.

"That's the wonderful thing about science. Sometimes the results you get are the ones you least expect."

Chapter Twelve

"Ready?"

Travis stuck his head into the bathroom for the tenth time.

"Almost."

Rory finished putting on the earrings and stepped back. She'd almost dropped the pretty diamond teardrops down the sink, her hands shook so badly. Why in the world had she agreed to let Willa host a reception to introduce her work? And how in the world was she going to get through three hours of talking to strangers? She turned to Travis, who smiled at her from the doorway. He looked amazing in the charcoal gray suit. He'd even splurged and worn a tie. No matter how bad the evening turned out for her, she knew at least she was going home with the hottest man there.

"How do I look?" She twirled in front of him. The silver and black silk dress hit her knees with a half-train further down in the back. It made her feel like a princess.

"You really need to ask me that? You can't tell from the fact that I'm drooling here?"

"It's more that I really need to hear it from you in words. Drool can be discounted as other things." Rory placed a hand on her stomach. "I think I'm going to be sick."

"No, you're not. What you're going to be is

lavished with praise, adored and admired, talked about for years to come."

"Now you're making me more nervous. I've been trying to get people to stop talking about me."

"Ah, but this time it won't be gossip. They'll be telling you to your face how amazing you are and how much they love your work."

"Enough to buy it?"

"They'll be buying it like crazy. Willa won't be able to keep it on the shelves." Travis looked at his watch. "But if we don't leave now, you'll be making your grand entrance late. We've still got to stop and pick up Margaret."

"It was nice of you to offer to pick her up."

"You're the one who made sure she got an invitation and hounded her until she said yes." Travis leaned down and kissed her on the nose. "I think you picked up my persuasion techniques very well."

"I don't want her to feel like she's alone anymore. Now that the sheriff got the forensics report back and she knows once and for all that Laurel's dead, I'm hoping she can put the past in the past and not let it haunt her anymore."

"Speaking of hauntings, the Paranormal Posse wants another night out here. They were more than a bit disappointed to miss out on finding their ghost girl."

"I figured they might have been." Rory sighed. "Guess I'll have to let them set up in the bedroom this time to make up for it, huh?"

"I'm still not sure you should encourage them."

"Hey, you should be the one encouraging them. You're the head ghost hunter now."

Travis groaned. "Don't say things like that. I'm

already having to hide from Jane Harvitz."

"Really?"

"Word got around about the whole thing. Now she's after me to talk at another meeting about what it's like to be a reformed skeptic."

"And is that what you are?'

He stared down at her with a look Rory had been waiting her whole life to see in someone's eyes.

"What I am is the man who's going to walk into that reception tonight knowing I have the most beautiful woman in the world beside me. Ghosts, goblins, hell, fairy queens can come along if they want. So long as you're there with me I can tackle the natural, the supernatural, the dead, and the undead. I'm not going anywhere without you, Ms. DuMont, so bring it on. I can take it."

Rory wrapped her arms around him, loving the feel of having him close to her. She stood on tiptoes and planted a long hot kiss on his lips. It might have been a mistake because she had to resist the urge to slip her hands under his jacket and touch his skin. She wanted to touch him all over and have him return the favor. By the time she stepped back from the kiss they were both out of breath. She gazed up at him with a twinkle in her eyes.

"That's all good to hear. Cause you're gonna love what I've got planned for Beltane."

A word from the author...

I've been writing for as long as I can remember. Being a writer is more than something I do. It is the way I see the world, the way I process it. I believe in the power of stories. They make us smile, make us think, and give us untold moments of enjoyment. My stories come from the landscape around me and the worlds I build in my head. I am proud to be a storyteller, and I hope my work leaves you both satisfied and entertained.